The Church

The Body Of Christ

Grace D. Balogun

The Church -The Body of Christ
By Grace Dola Balogun

Copyright ©2014 Grace Dola Balogun

Contact Author at:
www.Gracereligiousbookspublishers.com
1-646-559-2533

Grace Religious Books Publishing & Distributors books may be ordered through booksellers or by contacting the publisher:

Grace Religious Books Publishing & Distributors, Inc.
New York
213 Bennett Avenue
New York, NY 10040

not necessarily reflect the views of the publisher, and the publisher hereby disclaims any responsibility for them.

The author of this book does not dispense medical advice or prescribe the use of any technique as for treatment for physical, emotional, or medical problems without the advice of a physician, either directly or indirectly. The intent of the author is only to offer information of a general nature to help you in your quest for emotional and spiritual well-being. In the event you use any of the information in this book for yourself, which is your constitutional right, the author and the publisher assume no responsibility for your actions.

Soft Cover ISBN: 97819394115585
Hard Cover ISBN: 9781939415592

Library of Congress Control Number: 2014904486

Editing and Interior Design by CBM Christian Book Marketing www.christian-book-marketing.com

Cover Design by Lisa Hainline www.lisahainline.com

Printed in the United States of America
Grace Religious Books Publishing & Distributors, Inc.
New York

"God, the firstborn over all creation. For by him all things were created; things in heaven and on earth, visible and invisible, whether thrones or powers or rulers or authorities; all things were created by him and for him. He is before all things, and in him all things hold together. And he is the head of the body, the church; he is the beginning and the firstborn from among the dead, so that in everything he might have the supremacy. For God was pleased to have all his fullness dwell in him, and through him to reconcile to himself all things, whether things on earth or things in heaven, by making peace through his blood, shed on the cross"(Colossians 1:15-20).

Dedication

I dedicate this book to our Lord Jesus Christ who is the head of the Church. We are His body, His flesh and His bone. Jesus Christ came to this world to redeem all those who will believe in Him from their past, present, and future sins. Christ is our sin bearer and our Great Intercessor in Heaven. Christ, our hope of glory, is coming back to judge the quick and the dead. All eyes shall see Him.

I also dedicate this book to all those who are going to read this book and put their faith and trust in the Lord Jesus Christ, making Him their Lord and Savior, surrendering all to His Lordship.

"For in Christ all the fullness of the Deity lives in bodily form, and you have been given fullness in Christ who is the head over every power and authority. In him you were also circumcised, in the putting off of the sinful nature, not with a circumcision done by the hands of men but with the circumcision done by Christ, having been buried with him in baptism and raised with him through your faith in the power of God, who raised him from the dead" (Colossians 2: 9-12).

Preface

The Church according to our Lord Jesus Christ is not a building, but it consists of all those who believe in Christ, who follow Him, surrender their life to Him and follow His teaching, as well as obeying His commandments. On the day of our Lord's ascension - the day in which our Lord was taken up to Heaven in the bodily presence of five-hundred and twenty people. including eleven of His apostles - because Judas Iscariot left them and hanged himself on the tree for betraying the Lord. The truth of Jesus Christ's resurrection is maintained and it is the great evidence of His divinity. Christ walked and talked with the apostles after His resurrection. He also ate with them on one occasion. He showed them again and again the marks of His wounds in His hands and in His feet, and His side where they pierced Him. For a good forty days after our Lord's resurrection from the grave, Christ instructed them (the apostles) on what they have to do. He gave them commandments through the Holy Spirit. He told them that the Holy Spirit, the comforter, will be the commander and instruct them about or concerning the doctrine they must preach. Christ spoke to the apostles on the day of His ascension about the things that pertaining to the Kingdom of God, as a kingdom of grace in the world of sin, and of the glory of God. He prepared them to receive the Holy Spirit so that they could be able to do their assignment that was designed for them to do. This was one of the proofs of Christ Jesus' resurrection because He showed Himself to the apostles and He was with them in and out for forty days. The Disciples knew quite well that this was their Master and Lord. Jesus Christ, especially by His words that he said to them, spoke to the Disciples plainly, clearly and authoritatively about the things pertaining to the Kingdom of God. Christ commanded them to wait for the blessing of the Holy Spirit. "On one occasion, while he was eating with them, he gave them this command: "Do not leave Jerusalem, but wait for the gift my Father promised, which you have heard me speak about. For John baptized with water, but in a few days you will be baptized with the Holy Spirit" (Acts 1:4-5). They must wait till the appointed time, which is not many days according to our Lord.

Likewise, believers must exercise hope, strong faith in promises of the Lord, in due time mercies of our Lord will come but with patience; the apostles had to wait at the particular appointed place which is in Jerusalem, where Christ was humiliated and put to shame, but now God the Father will exalt Him with the honor due Him, to teach us to forgive our enemies and those who persecuted us. With this favor, the apostles must now put on public character so that the light of the Lord may shine upon them when the Holy Spirit descends upon them in the same Jerusalem where their Lord was crucified.

The blessing of the Lord shall come and they will be baptized with the Holy Spirit. Christ breathed upon them the Holy Spirit while He was on Earth (John 20:22) and they were alive, baptism of the Holy Spirit shall have larger measures of the gift of graces and comfort, they shall be cleansed and purified by the power of the Holy Spirit as in the Old Testament when the priests were consecrated to the sacred function in the synagogues.

With this power of the Holy Spirit, the apostles will be more effectual than ever before; they will be more engaged to the Lord. They shall be tied to Christ, in that they will never forsake Him. The gift of the Holy Spirit baptism is the promise of the Father, which they had from Jesus Christ. The Holy Spirit was given by promise, the Spirit of God the Father is not given as the Spirit of men is given to men, the Spirit of God is given by the Word of

God, so that the gift may be more valuable, more sure and more of grace and which may be received by faith. It was the spirit of Jesus Christ, the promise of the Father, Jesus Christ's Father; who is also our Father. He is also the Father of all mercies, the sustainer of all things. The promise of the Father the apostles heard again and again from Jesus Christ, many, many times Christ assured the apostles that the comforter will come, which confirms the promise of God the Father.

The baptizing of the Holy Spirit makes all the believing Christians one with the Father, Son and the Holy Spirit. This makes us the body of Jesus Christ, and the Church of Jesus Christ, the visible or the invisible church on the Day of Pentecost, marking the beginning of the Church of Christ on Earth.

O God, our Savior, who wills that all should be saved and come to the knowledge of the truth, prospers your servants who labor in distant lands. Protect them in all perils by land and sea and air; support them in loneliness and in the hour of trial; give them grace and bear faithful witness to you, and endue them with burning zeal of love that they may turn to righteousness and finally obtain a crown of glory, through Jesus Christ, our Lord. Amen
(Scottish Book of Common Prayer, 1912)

TABLE OF CONTENTS

The Church's one foundation is Jesus Christ her Lord. She is His new creation, by water and the Word; from Heaven He came and sought her to be His holy bride; with His own blood He bought her, and for her life He died. Elect from every nation, yet one over all the Earth, her charter of salvation: one Lord, one faith, one birth one holy name she blesses, partakes one holy food, and to one hope she presses with every grace endued.

(Words of Samuel J. Stone, 1866)

"Let the peace of Christ rule in your hearts, since as members of one body you were called to peace. And be thankful. Let the word of Christ dwell in you richly as you teach and admonish one another with all wisdom, and as you sing psalms, hymns and spiritual songs with gratitude in your hearts to God. And whatever you do, whether in word or deed, do it all in the name of the Lord Jesus, giving thanks to God the Father through him"(Colossians 3:15-17).

Chapter One

On The Day of Pentecost

The gift that the Father promised the Son right from the Book of Joel in the Old Testament (Joel 2:28-29 & Matthew 3:11): "When the day of Pentecost came, they were all together in one place. Suddenly a sound like the blowing of a violent wind came from heaven and filled the whole house where they were sitting. They saw what seemed to be tongues of fire that separated and came to rest on each of them. All of them were filled with the Holy Spirit and they began to speak in other tongues as the Spirit enabled them"(Acts 2:1-4). All the apostles had been waiting for the promise of the Father through Jesus Christ. They waited in the city of Jerusalem and they continued to pray individually and in groups. The Lord Jesus Christ fulfilled His promise of the Father to the Church on the Day of Pentecost. On this blessed day, in the history of the Church, marked the beginning of the Church of Jesus Christ on Earth, which our Lord said to Peter, during His earthly ministry when He was with them, "And I tell you that you are Peter, and on this rock I will build my church, and the gates of Hades will not overcome it" (Matthew 16:18). Christ promised to build His Church when He was on Earth; He promised to build His Church on the truth of Peter's words and the other apostles, including those who will believe in Him after the apostles.

The Church of Christ will be built on the confession of the truth that revealed Jesus Christ as the true Son of the living God - Christ will build His church on Peter's solid confession of Christ: Jesus is the rock, the foundation of the Church, the living stone, which was chosen and precious where all the believing Christians are the living stones who become part of the structure of the spiritual house that God the Father Himself builds. Jesus Christ promised that His church is going to be built and nothing in all creation can stop it.

Pentecost was the second great festival of the Jewish year. It was always the harvest festival when the first fruits of the grain harvest were presented to God.

"From where ever you live, bring two loaves made of two tenths of an ephah of fine four, baked with yeast, as a wave offering of the first fruits to the Lord. From the day after the Sabbath, the day you brought the sheaf of the wave offering, count off seven full weeks. Count off fifty days up to the day after the Seventh Sabbath, and then present an offering of new grain to the Lord" (Leviticus 23:15-17). The Scripture revealed that in the Old Testament there are festivals of seven full weeks, which was called the Feast of Weeks which is also called the Feast of Pentecost, which occurred at the end of the Wheat Harvest, which is 50-days, whereby Pentecost means "fifty" after the feast of first fruits. On this day God's people gave thanks for His abundant gifts of food and for all that sustained them throughout that year. It was a Day of Pentecost that God poured out the Holy Spirit on Christ's followers, the Disciples and on those who are with them. Therefore, in like manner, Pentecost symbolizes for the Church the beginning of God's harvest of souls in the world.

The Day of Pentecost marks the Harvest of God the Father's work of redemption of all the humanity in the world, but first for the Disciples and those who were present on that day. Pentecost gave the people of this world three observable manifestations of the Holy Spirit. The

Holy Spirit descended upon one hundred and twenty people; the Disciples and those who are the followers of Jesus Christ who believe in Him, and in the fulfillment of the Holy Spirit.

The Scripture further reveals that there was an <u>audible manifestation</u> of the Holy Spirit, which means there was a sound like a rushing of violent wind; as a prophetic sign that the Holy Spirit was coming in power. Winds are one of the Biblical symbols of the Holy Spirit. Our Lord said: "In reply Jesus declared, 'I tell you the truth, no one can see the Kingdom of God unless he is born again. The wind blows wherever it pleases. You hear its sound, but you cannot tell where it comes from or where it is going. So it is with everyone born of the Spirit" (John 3:3, 8). The Spirit is like wind, though unseen, is identified by its activities and sound; it is the same with the Holy Spirit.; It is observed by his activity and its effect on all those who are born again Christians.

<u>The visual manifestation</u>: The Holy Spirit also appeared visible which means the sign that seems to be tongues of fire that rested on each of the Disciples as a prophetic symbol that the Holy Spirit was coming to empower them in fiery, contagious witnesses for Jesus. "But you will receive power when the Holy Spirit comes on

you; and you will be my witnesses in Jerusalem, and in all Judea and Samaria and to the ends of the earth" (Acts 1:8). Our Lord Jesus, before He ascended to Heaven told the apostles that the primary purpose of the baptism in the Spirit is the receiving of power to witness that is from Jesus Christ, so that the sinner and the lost will be converted over to Him and taught to obey all that Christ commanded. At the end, so that Christ may be known, loved, praised and made the Lord of God's chosen people.

The Speech Manifestation: All the Disciples and other followers were being filled with the Holy Spirit; they began to speak in other tongues as the Spirit enabled them. On this particular day, there were a variety of native languages understood by the different nations represented in the crowd. "Then how is it that each of us hears them in his own native language? Parthians, Medes and Elamites; residents of Mesopotamia, Judea and Cappadocia, Pontus and Asia, and Pamphylia, Egypt and the parts of Libya near Cyrene; visitors from Rome, both Jews and converts to Judaism: Cretans and Arabs we hear them in our own tongues!" (Acts 2:8-11). The Spirit gave the power to the apostles to speak in different foreign languages spoken supernaturally by the Galilean Disciples were a corporate prophetic sign that the witness of the Church was to be universal to the end of the world.

The three observable manifestations at Pentecost correspond exactly to the three forces promised of the risen Lord to His Disciples in concerning the power to witness to all the people in the world. On that Day of Pentecost, the Disciples knew that their Master, Jesus Christ, was fulfilling His word of promise from His ascended position at the right hand of God in Heaven. Christ the ascended, exalted Lord and Christ at the right hand of the Father in whom all authority belongs. "Exalted to the right hand of God, he has received from the Father the promised Holy Spirit and has poured out what you now see and hear. Therefore, let all Israel be assured of this: God has made this Jesus, whom you crucified, both Lord and Christ" (Acts 2: 33, 36).

The outpouring of the Holy Spirit by Jesus proves that He is indeed the exalted Messiah, now sitting at the right hand of God and interceding for His representatives on Earth. After Jesus' baptism and onward, the Spirit was fully on Him as the Christ, the Messiah, and the Anointed One by the Holy Spirit. Now the same Christ, now at the right hand of God, He ever lives to pour out the same Holy Spirit on those who believe in Him. Pouring out the Holy

Spirit as Jesus Christ intends, the Holy Spirit will mediate Jesus' Presence to all the believing Christians and empower them to continue to do all that Christ did while He was on Earth. Filled with the Holy Spirit, the importance and the significance of the filling with the Holy Spirit at Pentecost means that the beginning of the fulfillment of God's promise in "And afterward, I will pour out my Spirit on all people. Your sons and daughters will prophesy, your old men will dream dreams, your young men will see vision. Even on my servants, both men and women, I will pour out my Spirit in those days" (Joel 2:28-29). Prophet Joel predicts a day when God would pour out His Spirit on everyone who calls on the name of the Lord. This outpouring will result in a charismatic flow of the Spirit and prophetic manifestations among God's people. Apostle Peter quoted this passage on the Day of Pentecost explaining that the outpouring of the Holy Spirit on that day was the beginning of the fulfillment of Joel's prophecy. This prophecy is an ongoing promise to all who accept Jesus Christ as Lord, for all believers can and should be filled with the Holy Spirit. Prophet Joel's visions says that one of the primary results of the outpouring of the Holy Spirit will be the impartation and the release of the prophetic gifts. The manifestation of the Holy

Spirit through His gifts makes known God's presence among His people. The Scripture revealed that word to Apostle Paul: "But if an unbeliever or someone who does not understand comes in while everybody is prophesying, he will be convinced by all that he is a sinner and will be judged by all, and the secrets of his heart will be laid bare. So he will fall down and worship God, exclaiming, 'God is really among you!' " (1st Corinthians 14: 24-25).

This is evidence of the surest at work in any congregational church is the conviction of sin, righteousness and judgment. Through the manifestation of the Holy Spirit among God's people, sin will be exposed, repentance called for, and sinners were convicted. We have to know that where there is no exposing of unrighteousness, no conviction of sin, and no pleading for repentance, the Holy Spirit will clearly not be at work according to the biblical pattern. The exposing of sin within a person's heart does not require a special gift of revelation, or mind searching the word of prophecy and its moral truth when proclaimed under the impulse of the Spirit is sufficient to convict the sinner's heart. Everyone on Earth is now confronted with the decision to repent and believe in Jesus Christ.

"For God so loved the world that he gave his only Son, so that everyone who believes in him may not perish but may have eternal life" (John 3:16). This is the number one verse in the Bible and more memorized by believers, unbelievers and people of all other religions. This verse continues to be memorized more than any other verses in the Scripture because in a few words it tells the story of salvation; God's love for the people in the world; God's gift of his Son, and the witness to whoever believes to be saved.

Chapter Two

God's People in Christ

God's people who gave their life to Jesus Christ are called, bound together as the citizens of God's Kingdom. They are always together for the purpose of worship, as well as listening to the Word of God through the Scripture. Churches can be seen everywhere as a local church either large of small. The people who belong to Jesus Christ are the Church or are also called the universal church: The Scripture revealed, " Consequently, you are no longer foreigners and aliens, but fellow citizens with God's people and members of God's household, build on the foundation of the apostles and prophets, with Christ Jesus himself as the Chief Cornerstone" (Ephesians 2:19-20). The church can only be a true church if it is founded on the Jesus Christ inspired in fallible revelation to the first apostle. The apostles were the first laborers and missionaries, as well as messenger's, eye-witnesses and authorized representatives of our crucified and risen Lord. They were the foundational stones of the Church, and their messages were presented in the writings of the New Testament as the original, fundamental testimony of the Gospel of Jesus Christ, which is valid and we are studying, reading preaching, and continue to witness for all times at all times, till this moment in time. All Christian's believers and churches are dependent on the words, message and faith of the first apostles as recorded in the Book of Acts of apostles and in their inspired New Testament books. From generation to generations the Church of Christ has the task of obeying the New Testament revelation and of bearing witness to the truth of the Gospel. The Gospel that was given to the New Testament apostles through the Holy Spirit is the enduring source of life, truth and direction for the Church. All the believing Christians and churches are true believers and true churches only so long as they do the following important things. They must in sincerity of agreement with a sincere heart strive to follow the New Testament book in the teaching and revelation concerning Jesus Christ and the gospel of God.

"Every day they continued to meet together in the temple courts. They broke bread in their homes and ate together with glad and sincere hearts" (Acts 2:46). Believers must not reject the apostles teaching, to reject the apostle teaching is like rejecting the Lord himself. "They devoted themselves to the apostles' teaching and to the fellowship, to the breaking of bread and to prayers" (Acts 2:42).

The Scripture further revealed seven important ways that believers of Jesus Christ must be devoted to the Lord and to themselves; it describes important characteristic of a Spirit filled church on Earth. (a) Apostles teaching the early church believers were Disciples and nourished in the word taught by the apostle, some of which later became our New Testament Scriptures - they were the Word centered church - the Word of the Lord Himself. (b) Believers fellowship of disciples must develop a vertical relationship to God, but also touch horizontally a warm, honest, open, healing, redeeming fellowship based on a common life together in Christ. They pursued the fellowship of Christ and the Holy Spirit between and among the believer. (c) Breaking of bread - this common expression in the Book of Acts and the early church seems to have a threefold dimension - the initial beginning of a common meal, the moment of sharing in an agape meal, and the Lord's Supper itself. (d) Prayer: Prayer was one of the essential ways of togetherness in the early church. Prayer was clearly a high priority and an integral part of their life together. In the Book of Acts, where there is much prayer, there is much activity of the Holy Spirit, and were there is much activity of the Holy Spirit, and where there is much activity of the Holy Spirit there is much prayer. Prayer is the key, the tools; the ladder to Heaven, prayer is the bell of believers ringing when we kneel down praying to God. (e) Miracles and signs and wonders: Miracles are one of the important aspects of the presence and power of the Holy Spirit among the believers. They occurred most often in their mission to unbelievers. Here is an example of miracle of healing: "One day two apostles Peter and John were going up to the temple at the time of prayer at three in the afternoon. Now a man crippled from birth was being carried to the temple gate called Beautiful, where he was put every day to beg from those going into the temple courts. When he saw Peter and John about to enter, he asked them for money. Peter looked straight at him, as did John. Then Peter said, 'Look at us,' so the man gave them his attention, expecting to get something from them. Then Peter said, 'Silver or gold I do not have, but what I have I give you. In the name of Jesus Christ of Nazareth, walk,' taking him by the right hand, he helped him up, and instantly the man's feet and ankles became strong. He jumped to his feet and began to walk. Then he went with them into the temple courts, walking and jumping, and praising God. When all the people saw him walking and praising God, they recognized him as the same man who used to sit begging at the temple gate called Beautiful, and they were filled with wonder and amazement at what had happened to him" (Acts 3:1-10).

"They all joined together constantly in prayer, along with women and Mary the mother of Jesus and with his brothers" (Acts 1:14). The experience of Pentecost always involves human responsibility. Those who are in need of Holy Spirit's outpouring power to do the work of God should make themselves available to the Holy Spirit through the commitment of God's will through prayer.

We have to notice the parallelism between the Spirit coming on Jesus and the Spirit coming on the Disciples, that descended on them after they have prayed. These were the observable manifestations of the Holy Spirit ministries of Jesus and the Disciples beginning after the Spirit descended upon them with power on the Day of Pentecost. "Stretch out your hand to heal and perform miraculous signs and wonders through the name of your holy servant Jesus" (Acts 4: 30-31) after they prayed, the place where they were meeting was shaken. And they were all filled with the Holy Spirit and spoke the word of God boldly" Preaching and miracles belong together, miracles accompanying with signs by which Jesus Christ confirms the word of witnesses by miraculous signs which generally means the deeds performed in order to certify the existence of a divine power of the Holy Spirit, giving warnings or encouraging faith. "Wonders" refer to usual or very unusual events that cause the observers to marvel, or wonder. Churches of Jesus Christ pray that healing, miraculous signs and wonder to take place during their service of the Lord. This also will be happening at the last day and it will face the many challenges of the Last Days.

The present churches today need to pray earnestly that God in Jesus Christ will confirm the Gospel with great power from above, miracles and abundant grace can only happen when we proclaim the Gospel in the power of the New Testament witness that will be able to reach the sinner and the lost generation for Christ.

Where the apostles assembled together was shaken, this also is an important truth that stands forever. Baptism with or in the Holy Spirit describes the consecrating work of the Holy Spirit in initiating the believer into divine power for witness. The terms filled, or clothed and empowered describe the Holy "Spirit equipping the Saints for the work of the ministry as the need arises within the body of Christ the church. The Scripture also, revealed that: "The apostles performed many miraculous signs and wonders among the people and all the believers used to meet together in Solomon's Colonnade, crowds gathered also from the towns around Jerusalem, bringing their sick and those tormented by evil spirits, and all of them were healed" (Acts 5:12, 16). Apostles healed all the people that came to them. They did same thing as their Lord did during His earthly ministry. Apostles healed the sick and delivered those that were tormented with evil spirits. This showed a great sign; it was very paramount that the Kingdom of God had come among the people with great power. It is part of the sign of the full message of a new life in Christ; that God by the Holy Spirit working through all the believers desires to heal those who are sick oppressed, and disabled. We also have the Scriptures which say: "Now Stephen, a man full of God's grace and power, did great wonders and miraculous signs among the people" (Acts 6:8). The Holy Spirit empowered Stephen to perform great wonders and miraculous signs among the people and gave him great wisdom to preach the gospel of God in such a way that they people could not refute his arguments of the Scriptures. "When the crowds heard Philip and saw the miraculous signs he did, they all paid close attention to what he said" (Acts 8:6). Christ Jesus promised those who believe in Him with the use of miraculous signs to confirm the preaching and teaching of the word of God was not limited to the apostles alone, but was also opened to those who will follow them by believing in Jesus Christ. Christ promises that the disciples' converts and whoever believes, sinners and the lost. All those who are converted will perform signs in the name of Jesus Christ, such as driving out demons and healing the people with diverse diseases which is exactly what Philip did on that day to the people who are in hearing and in his reach. (f) Sharing community: All the people in this world are made for life in the community with God. The people or Christians in the early church in Jerusalem experienced community just like few people have in the world. "All the believers were one in heart and mind. No one claimed that any of his possessions was his own, but they shared everything they had. With great power the apostles continued to testify to the resurrection of the Lord Jesus and much grace was upon them all (Acts 4: 32-33).

Great power is the distinguishing characteristic of the apostolic preaching, teaching and witnessing. Therefore, because of this reason, apostolic witness was based on the Word of God. They prayed that, "Now, Lord, consider their threats and enable your servants to speak your word with great boldness" (Act 4:29). The Disciples needed the renewed courage to witness and speak clearly and boldly about Christ. It is the same with all the believers today; we must speak boldly clearly about Jesus Christ and about the gospel of God throughout our Christian life. We need to pray constantly without ceasing in order to overcome our fear of embarrassment, rejection, criticism or persecution. God's grace, through the fillings of the Holy Spirit, will help us to speak about our Lord Jesus Christ with great boldness throughout our life (g) making disciples: The Scripture revealed that the apostles were: praising God and enjoying the favor of all the people and the Lord added to their number daily those who were being saved" (Acts 2: 47) The righteous influence and witness of these believers effectively permeated the city as they naturally overflowed of their life together and out flow of Jesus' ministry through the apostles by the Holy Spirit. Consequently, new converts were being added to the church daily through the power of the Holy Spirit.

The sin of jealousy over the blessings and achievements of others, especially the spiritual enjoyment and advance of the kingdom of Christ that is freely, and graciously, bestowed upon the people of Christ is evident in the Old Testament examples of the sin of jealousy that include the rival of Joseph's brothers over the favor that Joseph received at the hand of God. (Read More...Genesis 37:12-36)

Chapter Three

The Assembly

"The assembly was in confusion: some were shouting one thing, some another. Most of the people did not even know why they were there; if there is anything further you want to bring up, it must be settled in a legal assembly. After he had said this, he dismissed the assembly" (Acts 19:32, 39, and 41). The assembly in this particular time was unplanned and it was riotous within the body of Christ and the fellow citizens of the people. Christian believers must be separated and concentrated to the worship and service of God; the word church always means the people of God, Christ believers - Christians.

"He was in the assembly in the desert, with the angel who spoke to him on Mount Sinai, and without fathers; and he received living words to pass on to us" (Acts 7:38). The assembly in the desert refers to the people of Israel as the people of God. Just as Moses led the assembly of the Old Testament, Jesus Christ leads the assembly church of the New Testament. The New Testament Church were Abraham's seed in the continuity with the assembly of the Old Testament, just like the Old Testament assembly the Church of the New Testament in the desert can be seen as a pilgrim Church on a journey of faith to the Promised Land. Therefore, we must not be too comfortable with life here on Earth and remember this is a temporary habitation for the people of God.

"The Lord gave me two stone tablets inscribed by the finger of God. On them were all the commandments the Lord proclaimed to you on the Mountain out of the fire, on the day of the assembly (Deuteronomy 9:10). God wants us to know that the Israelites' possession of the land is not because of their righteousness and not a reward for their own past or present faithfulness, but it was God's gracious gift, which was based on His love and infinite mercy. Moses warned the people of Israel that continued possession meant perseverance in faith and in obedience to God of Abraham. "I will sprinkle clean water on you, and you will be clean; I will cleanse you from all your impurities and from all your Idols. I will give you a new heart and put a new Spirit in you; I will remove from your heart of stone and give you a new heart and put a new Spirit in you. I will remove from your heart the stone and give a heart of flesh. And I will put my Spirit in you and move you to follow my decrees and be careful to keep my laws" (Ezekiel 36: 25-27). God's plan to restore the people of Israel back to their land in order to show His power, His holiness, and His great name so all the nations of Earth will know that the God of Israel is the only one God and the only true God of all the people in the world. God's promises to the people of Israel and to the people in the world is His restoration in the lives of individuals physically and spiritually involves giving them a new heart that is tender as flesh so that they will respond to God's Word, and God's will; He will be able to put his Holy Spirit in them.

This is the work of God that encompasses the New Covenant, which Jesus Christ established. It is clear and precise that without the power of the indwelling of the Holy Spirit, it is impossible for a converted Christian or unconverted individual to have true life and follow the commandment of God, or live a holy life. It is very essential that we remain open and discern the voice and guidance of the Holy Spirit. "What agreement is there between the temple of God and Idols? For we are the temple of the living God. As God has said: I will live with them and walk among them, and I will be their God, and they will be my people" (2nd Corinthian 6:16).   The Scripture revealed that a born-again, converted individual or converted sinner is the temple of God, a place of habitation for the Holy Spirit. Idols in the Old Testament and the New Testament represented demons; idolatry worship of idols man made idols temples.

Christians must never desecrate their bodies as the Spirit's indwelling place, therefore allowing demonic access. We have to be confident that no evil spirit will live alongside the Holy Spirit within the true believing Christians, although there may unusual circumstances in which an evil spirit lives in an individual who is actively in the process of conversion may at times require the driving of demons from the individual person who sincerely desires to follow Christ. It is an underlying problem with that person's sins. In this type of incidence the person will not be able to experience full life of Christ and full life of salvation until there is full deliverance and completeness in Christ.

"Yet, before the twins were born or had done anything good or bad - in order that God's purpose in election might stand" (Romans 9:11). The Scripture is revealing to us that the problem of the people of Israel's election and rejection of the Gospel and their salvation, the Jewish converted Christians asking themselves how could God promise Abraham and his true descendents while the entire nation of Israel were not part of the Gospel? Apostle Paul maintains that God's promise to the people of Israel will never fail and has never failed. It was meant for the true and faithful Israelites; there are always a people of God within the nations who have received the promises of God in various ways, and in various times. God, the Creator, is the planner and orchestrator of the Universe. He has the right and power to do what he pleases with an individual and with the nations on Earth. God has the right to put aside and reject any nation who does not obey His commandment; God also has the right to have mercy upon those who need His mercy, and to who are obedient to His commandments and offer them the gift of salvation through the redemptive work of Jesus Christ. It is the same till today, not all that called the name of the Lord truly belong to Him. "I do not want you to be ignorant of this mystery, brothers, so that you may not be conceited: Israel has experienced a hardening in part until the full number of the Gentiles has come in. And so all Israel will be saved, as it is written; the deliverer will come from Zion he will turn godlessness away from Jacob, and this is my covenant with them when I take away their sins" (Romans 11:25-27). In this Scripture the full number of Gentiles signifies the completion of God's purpose in the work of redemption. God called the Gentiles from the people of the world, when their wickedness ws so plenty - when sin in the world grieved the Spirit of God, peoples' sin reached the level of so many rebellious attitudes against God.

The Church and the kingdom of God are related. Jesus Christ did not found or organize the Church, not until after His resurrection. Christ said to Peter: "Blessed are you, Simon son of Jonah! For flesh and blood has not revealed this to you, but my Father in heaven" (Matthew 16:17).

Chapter Four

Christ Will Judge the World

Christ comes to judge the world. At that time the number of Jewish people who believe in Christ will greatly increase during the dark days of tribulation. Tribulation will end when Christ brings deliverance to the believers in Israel and destroys the remaining unbelieving Jewish people. All the rebellious and ungodly Jews will be rooted out - the believing remnant of Israelites from past generations will constitute the nation of Israel. According to the Scripture: "Therefore, prophesy and say to them: This is what the Sovereign Lord says: O my people, I am going to open your graves and bring you up from them; I will bring you back to the land of Israel. Then you, my people, will know and bring you up from them. I will put my Spirit in you and you will live, and I will settle you in your own land. Then you will know that I the Lord have spoken, and I have done it, declares the Lord" (Ezekiel 37: 12-14).

This Scripture revealed the love of God to the people of Israel even though they were very disobedient to God's commandment, but His love for them never fails. This vision of the Prophet Ezekiel revived bones would be fulfilled at the time of the children of Israel's restoration, which will be both physically and spiritually. This restoration was initially fulfilled in the time of King Cyrus', but it will be fully realized when God gathers all the Israelites to their land in the end time and with great spiritual awakening. Many Jewish people will believe in Jesus Christ and will accept Jesus Christ as their Messiah before Christ returns to Earth to set up and establish His kingdom. "And I tell you that you are Peter, and on this rock I will build my church and the gates of Hades will not overcome it. I will give you the keys of the Kingdom of heaven, whatever you bind on earth will be bound in heaven, and whatever you loose on earth will be loosed in heaven" (Matthew 16: 18-19).

Our Lord was telling Peter that the gate of Hades will not overcome His work on Earth. The gate lof Hades represent all the demons and evil strategy that Satan can plan, or marshal in an attempt to destroy the Church or to withstand its mission in the world. It doesn't meant one particular believing Christians, it means all the Christians in the world from their household to local churches, fellowship of churches, or denominations will never fall away in any doctrinal errors or otherwise be overcome by sin or Satan's devices or snares.

Christ Jesus Himself warned all believing Christians and churches of possible spiritual deceptions and failures. It means that in spite of Satan's worst activities and plans of evil, the body of Christ, the Church that Jesus Christ is building, cannot be shaken or destroyed at the end. God's true church will rise up in faith, authority and in the power of the Holy Spirit to righteously destroy Satan's kingdom and domain of darkness by delivering people from their sins, disease, bondage and oppression. The body of Christ – the Church that Jesus is building and continues to build can never be destroyed, nor be successfully resisted by Satan. God's Kingdom is to be entered - the keys represent authority for entry - keys are also related to binding and loosing; Jesus Christ, to whom the Father gave all the authority in Heaven and on Earth, delegated His authority, which was represented by the keys Apostle Peter and the

Church of the believing Christians for carrying out the Great Commission.

Six days later, Jesus took with him, Peter and James and his brother John and led them up a high mountain, by themselves. And he was transfigured before them, and his face shone like the sun, and his clothes became dazzling white" (Matthew 17:1-2). Here we see three of Jesus' Disciples observed a great scene of God's approving of His Son Jesus, Moses whom God gave the Ten Commandments, together with Elijah, a great prophet, both appeared with Jesus and God the Father spoke from Heaven.

Chapter Five

All Authority Belongs to Christ

All authority belongs to Jesus Christ in Heaven and on this Earth. This authority for proclaiming the Gospel includes His delegated authority to bind and loose on Earth. In the Spirit - filled proclamation of the Gospel, the Church has been given the keys - authority to bind demons and diseases and to loose the prisoners of sin, addictions and sickness from their bondage and captivity unto salvation in the same way Jesus Christ did during His earthly ministry. The binding and loosing is an ongoing accomplishment and provision because Jesus Christ has finished the work on the Cross, which is now released on Earth through the Church to those who believe and will believe in Jesus Christ unto salvation of souls.

These keys which is the authority could also be used in church discipline within the body of Christ. According to the Scripture, we have an invisible church and visible church within the body of Christ. The invisible church is the body of true believing Christians that are united by their faith in Christ, loved the Lord and are very active in the service of the Lord: physically and spiritually. The visible church are the many local congregations containing faithful overcomers; they are those people who professed to be Christians by mouth but not by heart, they are false Christians; Christ did not know them. They are spiritually dead and lukewarm. "So Peter was kept in prison but the church was earnestly praying to God for Him" (Acts 12:5). The early church called themselves believers, disciples, saints, church, assembly - until the Gospel spread to Antioch did Jesus' followers begin to be called Christians most likely from the people of Antioch who were not believers.

Church gain in sight of authoritative standards - the church consists of people who formed local congregations and united by the Holy Spirit diligently seeking a faithful personal relationship with God the Father, Jesus Christ and the Holy Spirit. Through the power of the Holy Spirit, sinners will be saved, born again, baptized in water and added to the Church; they will begin a new life in Christ Jesus; from then on they will partake of the Lord's Supper and wait for Christ, their Lord's, return. The baptism in the Holy Spirit will be preached and communicated to the New Converted believers and the Spirit's presence and power will be manifested upon them. The Holy Spirit will be in operations including wonders, miracles signs and healing through the power of the Holy Spirit.

"Indeed, God did not send the Son into the world to condemn the world, but in order that the world might be saved through him. Those who believe in him are not condemned; but those who do not believe are condemned already, because they have not believed in the name of the Son of God" (John 3:17-18).

Chapter Six

Christ's Five Fold Instruction of Leadership

God gave a fivefold instruction of leadership to the Church in order to equip the Saints and for the work of the ministry. (1) Believing Christians will be empowering by the Holy Spirit to drive demons out of the people of this world through the power of the indwelling of the Holy Spirit. (2) There must be absolute loyalty to the Gospel, the original teachings of Jesus Christ and the apostles. Christian believers must devote themselves to studying and obeying the Word of God. (3) On the first day of the week the local congregation will meet together for worship and mutual edification through the written word of God and the manifestations of the Spirit. (4) The church will stand in humility, awe and fear before the presence of a Holy God. The people will be vitally concerned for the purity of the Church - the body of Christ. Disciplining the members who fall unto sin and teaching not loyal to the Biblical faith. (5) Those who persevered in a godly character and living righteously within the standard set forth by the Church will be ordained as elders to oversee that the local church congregation are maintaining their spiritual life. It is the same with the deacons who are responsible for the temporary, material affairs of the Church. (6) There must be observable love and fellowship in the Spirit among the members not only within the local congregation, but also between other Bible believing Christian's congregations. (7) The Christian must be praying and fasting from time to time in order to be strengthening in the Lord. (8) Believing Christians must separate themselves from the prevailing world view and the Spirit of their surrounding culture. (9) There will be suffering and affliction because of the world. (10) The Church must actively be sending the laborer into the missions field to all other nations.

The Church must also engage in a prolonged corporate prayer, fervent prayer of any situations that are looking impossible just as the early Church lived by the conviction that prayer of a righteous man is powerful and its effect is that it can move mountains. They prayed intensely and steadily, unceasing over Peter's situation. Their prayer was answered and the angel of the Lord went and release Peter from prison. It is the same today, the Christian believers church – the body of Christ, must engaged in prolonged corporate prayer. God intends His children to gather together for meaningful enduring prayers. Jesus Said: My house will always be called a house of prayer" (Matthew 21:13). Churches must be based on their theology, practice and mission on the practice of fervent corporate prayer as a vital element of their worship and not just one or two minutes in service.

Now there was a Pharisee named Nicodemus, a leader of the Jews. He came to Jesus by night and said to him, "Rabbi, we know that you are a teacher who came from God; for no one can do these signs that you do apart from the presence of God." Jesus answered him very truly, I tell you, no one can see the kingdom of God without being born from above" (John 3:1-4).

Chapter Seven

Power of Prayer as the Church- the Body

During the early church, God's power and presence and prayer meetings went together. There is no amount of preaching, teaching, singing that must be done or any activity that will bring forth the genuine power and presence of the Holy Spirit, without prayer where believers joined together constantly in prayer. Take a look at the Temple of God according to the Scripture: He brought me to the Portico of the temple and measured the jams of the portico; they were five cubits wide on either side. The width of the entrance was fourteen cubits and its projecting walls were three cubits wide on either side. The portico was twenty cubits wide on either side. The portico was twenty cubits wide, and twelve cubits from front to back. It was reached by flight of stairs and there were pillars on each side of the jams" (Ezekiel 40:48). "On the twenty - first day of the seven month the word of the Lord came through the prophet Hagai, 'Speak to Zerubbabel son of Shealtiel, governor of Judah, to Joshua son of Jehozadak, the High Priest. Be strong, all you people of the land, declares the Lord, and work. For I am with you, declares the Lord Almighty. This is what I covenanted with you when you came out of Egypt. And my Spirit remains among you. Do not fear. This is what the Lord Almighty says: In a little while I will once more I will shake the heavens and the earth, the sea and the dry land. I will shake all nations, and the desired of all nations will come, and I will fill this house with glory, says the Lord Almighty. The silver is mine and the gold is mine, declares the Lord Almighty. The glory of this present house will be greater than the glory of the former house, says the Lord Almighty, and in this place I will grant peace declares the Lord Almighty (Hagai 2:1-9).

The Scripture is telling us about the visitation of the Lord God Almighty to the people of the Earth when He is ready to establish a new order of the Universe. It also, refers to God's Judgment at the end of the age in the world, which will precede and accompany Christ's return to Earth. The Earth and sky will tremble; God's glory will then fill the temple more than ever before, and He will dwell among His people in peace as the glorious Savior and Lord of all people in the world. Just as in the Book of Joel, in the Book of Leviticus and the Book of Acts, chapter two verses 16-36 in which Apostle Peter revealed on the Day of Pentecost. "Therefore, I urge you, brothers, in view of God's mercy, to offer your bodies as living sacrifices, holy and pleasing to God - this is your spiritual act of worship. Do not conform any longer to the pattern of this world, but be transformed by the renewing of your mind. Then you will be able to test and approve what God's will is, his good, pleasing and perfect will" (Romans 12: 1-2).

Because of God's profound mercy to all the believers in Jesus Christ, all should be willing to offer their bodies to God as a living sacrifices for His honor, praises and glory. A believing Christians' greatest desire should be to live lives of Holy worship and devotion to God; which requires separating themselves from all the earthly lust and anything that can contaminate spirit, soul or body. Believers must pursing God in holy passion and focus. Believer' bodies are to be consecrated to God for a lifetime of worship and service. Believers must offer their bodies as dead to sin, instruments of righteousness and as the temple of the Holy Spirit. Believers must not conform to the pattern of this world or this present world system and must not squeeze into its mold on many different levels. True believers must firmly resist the lust of the eye in the world, resist conforming to the present world system under the Satan's rule which is hostile to God and his people, which is built on human wisdom and values; as well as built on an unbiblical world view. The kingdom of Jesus Christ is not of this world. The world system under Satan is full of darkness, deception and seduction with all sexual immoralities. Believers are called to the light in the middle of darkness. Believers are also exhorted in the Scripture to resist temptation and to yield, and not to conform to, the many forms of worldliness surrounding the body of Christ, which is the church. They must resist greed, self-centered living, principles of expediency, humanistic thinking, political maneuvering for power, envy, hatred, revenge, impurity and lust, filthy language, ungodly entertainment, immorality, drugs, worldly companions and unrighteous things, or unrighteous living.

The alternative to conforming to the world's values and lifestyle is transformation. Transformation results when Jesus Christ and His Word renew our minds so that our vision, values and plans are governed by God's revelation and eternal truth, rather than by the world's temporal and deceptive pattern. Believers having a renewed mind and living a transformed life in Christ, will be able to test, prove and affirm that God's will is good, desirable and perfect. Transformed believers must know and embrace God's will as the highest and best way of life.

The sacraments of the church are at the heart of the expression of the church's faith the sacraments of baptism and the Lord's Supper.   The former symbolized entrance into the church while the later provides spiritual sustenance for the church.   Baptism symbolizes the sinner's entrance into the church and become the church.   "Jesus answered, "I tell you the truth, no one can enter the kingdom of God unless he is born of water and the Spirit" (John 3:5).

Chapter Eight

Christs Priestly Prayer

Jesus Christ's prayers, His prayer during the time that He was saying farewell to His Disciples. It was a prayer offered after the sermon, when He had spoken from God to them, He turned and speaks to God about them and about us today. Those people we preach to, we must also pray for them. This was prayer after the sacraments communion - Christ prays that God the Father would preserve the good impressions of the ordinance upon the apostles. It was a family prayer to Christ's Disciples because they were His family, for three good years they have been together day and night. To set up a good example, Jesus Christ blessed His household, He prayed for them and with them. It was a farewell prayer. We Christian believers should copy Christ's love and pray for our friends, our relatives, our boss, etc. It was a prayer before His sacrifice of Himself as an atonement, which He was now about to offer on Earth. Jesus Christ prayed as a priest now offering sacrifice where prayer were to be made; prayer was the specimen of Christ's intercession which He still is offering for us up till today. He ever lives to make intercession for those who believe in Him. We have to notice Christ expression of His fervent desire, which he used in His priestly prayer. Jesus Christ, as the true Son of God, the only begotten Son of the Father, lifted up His eyes and said: "Father" our Lord and Savior in his prayer called God, Holy Father, righteous Father we should copy Christ in our prayers. Jesus Christ prayed for Himself first even though Christ as God the Son, but here as full human man, he prayed, and after prayer for Himself, He prayed for His Disciples, which He prayed more for the Disciples more than Himself. The Father glorified the Son on Earth, even during His suffering on the Cross. The Father justified but He also glorified the Son, even when He was crucified, He was also magnified, as well as glorified.

Jesus Christ conquered Satan and death, the thorns on His head, God the Father turned it to a gold crown. The Father also, glorified the Son when he raised Him from the dead. All those believing Christians, those that have received the adoption of Sons; if sanctified, then they will be glorified. Jesus Christ stated that "The hour has come," which means the hour of the Redeemer's death, which is also the house of the Redeemer's birth most remarkable hour, without doubt. This is the most critical, ever since the beginning of creation. Christ glorified the Father with conformity to the work that the Father assigned Him to do on Earth. Christ's power was revealed through the Father's glory. Christ, who has all the power and authority; in Heaven and on Earth is seated at the right hand of God the Father to rule. Christ is incontestable, is indisputable, in whom all the power in Heaven and on Earth are given. He is the only one who has the power to give eternal life to those who choose to believe in Him and have strong faith in Him

What is born of flesh is flesh, and what is of the Spirit is Spirit" (John 3:6) the baptism of the Old Testament initiated baptism, especially in its association of repentance of sin; the baptism of John anticipated Christian baptism. John administered the baptism of repentance in expectation of the baptism of the Holy Spirit and fire that only Messiah would exercise.

Chapter Nine

Origin of Christ's Power

The Origin of Jesus Christ's power is from God the Father. He empowered Him to do the work that He assigned for Jesus Christ to do. It is the same with us today. Jesus Christ empowered the apostles and all of us today, so that we can be able to do what He wants us to do for His glory. Without the power of the Spirit of God the Father from the Son, we cannot serve the Lord according to his will for our life. Jesus Christ has power over all flesh and over all of humanity; He is our mediator of a New Covenant, meditating between God and human kind. All other things on Earth are put under His feet. Our Lord Jesus Christ has all the power over the entire sinful race, any form of sin and the sinful nature; moreover, He has the power over all the judgment committed to Him by His power.

Through Jesus Christ we have access to the throne of grace, to come to with liberty to approach the throne of grace boldly and confidently; both Jews and the Gentiles were reconciled to God through Jesus Christ who is our peace and by the blood of Christ we are saved. Christ exercised and maintained exceeding greatness of God's power towards those who believe in Him, those who gave their life to him totally and completely.

Now, let us consider Christ's power to give eternal life to those who believe in Him; those that the Father gave Him, the immortal crown that will never fade away. How great is our Lord and how gracious and mighty He is. He sanctifies us in this world, and gave us a spiritual life, which is eternal life and brought grace and heaven in the soul of believers. The eternal life goal is to know God and worship him in the Spirit of holiness. The knowledge of God and Jesus Christ leads us to eternal life; it shows us the way to Heaven.

Our Lord and Savior prayed that the Father give Him the glory He had before the world began. Christ therefore, "Is before all things and by him all things consist and manifested." Christ prayed that the Father glorified

Him with His own self. Jesus Christ prays for those that the Father has given Him who receive the Gospel and believe in Christ. Christ prayed to the Father that all His powers, all the gifts of the Holy Spirit, all His graces, for His own glory in man's salvation, justification, and sanctification of all the believers is through the righteousness of God. He prayed that they should not be removed from the world by death, but preserved them, keep them, save them in this world, and take them out of all the troubles of this world, out of terror attack and violence.

Our Lord Jesus prayed and said: "Holy Father, keep those whom you have given me." Christ committed them to the care of God the Father as he was about to leave the world. Those people that God Almighty kept safe are the people that belong to His Son. Christ put them under the divine protection of God the Father where no evil can be fall them. This prayer of our Lord Jesus Christ has been a wonderful preservation of the gospel ministry and the gospel church in the universe till today. All the believing Christian needs is the power of God, not only to restore us into the state of His grace, but to keep us under His divine power.

The Holy Father takes care of all His children where ever they may be, or in any circumstances. Jesus

Christ prayed that the Father keep all those who believe in Him in the knowledge and fear, as well as in the profession and service of His Holy name; by His own power, in your holy hand, let Your holy name be the believers' strong tower, keep them from evil and out of evil, keep them away from sin, all the sin nature in the world as well as deliver them from all evils. Christ kept them safe while He was with them except Judas Iscariot, the son of perdition. We are weak and restless, we are spiritually powerless, only Jesus Christ with the power of the Holy Spirit can keep us safe, and control, direct and energize us, protect us, provide for our needs, guide us and keep us safe at all times.

Christ is the Good Shepherd, the Great Shepherd, and the Chief Shepherd for the preservation of the sheep. Jesus Christ completed His work on Earth. He was going back to the Father; He carried with Him the burden and concern for His own people, Disciples who are in the world, as it is still the same today. Christ is tenderly concerned for those who believe in Him, who are in the world. He is our Great Intercessor in Heaven, praying to the Father for what we need, and calling the Father about what we are going through for divine intervention in our lives. Jesus Christ is always the believing Christians joy. He wants us to rejoice, and He wants our joy to be full with

Christ. Christ's joy is everlasting. He wants us to build up our joy in Him with diligence, and to be able to have a perfect joy in Him, not in the material things of this world. Jesus Christ's ministry of intercession for believers is more than enough to fulfill our greater joy in Him; nothing more important than to know that Christ always appears in the presence of God the Father for us.

"Do not be astonished that I said to you, you must be born from above. The wind blows where it chooses, and you hear the sound of it, but you do not know where it comes from or where it goes" (John 3:7). The wind though is unseen, is identified by its activity and sound, so also the Holy Spirit is observed by his activity in and effect on those who are born again.

Chapter Ten

Christ Prayed For the Father's Love to Dwell on His Church

Christ prayed that the love of the Father to dwell on all the believers: that the love of the Father in Him to flow to all those who belong to Him, those who gave their life to Him. This is the greatest blessing in the world when the love of the Father, Son and the Holy Spirit rest upon the believers, children of God permanently forever from this Earth to Heaven. Our Lord, Jesus Christ, prayed that the Father should sanctify believers. He prayed the Father to sanctify us and through out to the end of our lives. The word of truth, divine revelation produce our sanctification, sanctification is the seed of our new birth and the food of our new life in Christ. Ministers, pastors, and the preachers, and the teachers of the Word of God are sanctified with the truth, our Lord prayed that the Father's gift of grace must be bestowed upon them. Jesus Christ, after praying for His Disciples, prayed for those who will believe in Him through the witnessing of the Disciples and those who will go out and fulfill the Great Commission, those who will believe in Jesus Christ through other servants of the Gospel and Christ.

Jesus Christ prayed not only for great and eminent believers, but he also prayed for the poor, the needy, the weak and the distressed, the unborn as well as other sheep, that nobody knows during that time; the other sheep might be the Gentiles. Christ Jesus prayed that all must be one in Him as He is one with the Father; and be perfect in Him, that they might be one body of Christ. Christ Jesus prayed that the Father should make all the believers one in Him, whatever age, race, those residing in distant places and those who are near, to be united with one accord, in Him as the head of the body the Church. He prayed that all the believers will be one in Spirit, one Lord, One Baptism, Father of all and in Him all, one faith.

Christ prayed that all the Christians might be knit together in the bond of love, peace, and with one heart. These prayers of Jesus Christ our Lord might not be completely fulfilled until all the Christians believers arrive in Heaven. Christians are one in some measure now as God the Father and Jesus Christ are one. They are united by a divine nature, by the power of divine grace of the Holy Spirit's divine counsels. There is one God, and one mediator between God and mankind, all those who are truly united to God and Jesus Christ who are one will be united to one another as the Creator and the Redeemer are one. Union with God is through Christ who says: "I in them and you are in me," that they may be perfect in one and complete in Him. All the believers are God's ambassadors, whose glory is shining throughout the world, the glory of God, which he shines upon them wherever they may be. The glory that the believers are part of the covenant with the Father was the glory, which the Father gave to the Redeemer King Jesus Christ and Christ confirmed it to the redeemed, which are in the world.

God gave them this gift so that they might be one as well as they might have the privilege of unity of Christ in them. The gift of the Holy Spirit which the Father gave to the Son, to be given to all those who believe in Him makes them one in Him and also engages them to the duty of unity. Christian believers have to consider that they have one God, one Jesus Christ, one hope of Heaven; they have the blessing of one mind, and one mouth to glorify God the

Father, Son and Holy Spirit. Believers and non-believers must know that this world's glory set men and women at variable; for if some be advanced others are down (eclipsed). The more believers are taken up with the glory of Jesus Christ which is given to them, the less desirous they will be of vain glory and worldly lust, and consequently, the less they will stay out of violence.

All the believing Christians must know why they believe in Christ and where, why they believe in Christ and His redemptive work of salvation. Christ's good will to the people in the world is that He is the Father's mind, who would have all people in the world to be saved. Therefore, this is desire, His will that the Great Commission be fulfilled, and that the gospel of God is preached and taught to the people in the entire world. No stone should be left untouched and turned, people must be convicted of their sins and repent and be converted to the Lord from this Earth to Heaven. Believers must do their utmost best to reach the people of this world with salvation. They should let the oneness be the evidence of the truth of Christianity and the means, key, tool of bringing non-believers to embrace the Gospel.

Unity will be revealed through the love of Christ in us and will make Christianity a more desirable religion in the world that embody Christian believers in one society and it will greatly promote Christianity in the world. The people in the world will see great changes in the life of the children of God, and the people of this world will follow Christ and His teaching and the power of his love to all mankind. The unity of all Christians show the beauty of their profession and will invite other nonbelievers to join them. They will see the love of God in Jesus Christ and be converted unto the Lord. It is a great privilege to know that the Father loved them with the same love that He loves His Son and that believers are loved with the Father's everlasting love; if we love one another with a pure heart. Our Lord prayed Father, "I will that they may be with me" our Lord prayed for believers' sanctification and now He prayed for their glorification. Christ prayed for believers with the authority of His intercession, His prayer was with power in Heaven, as well as on Earth.

"And John testified, I saw the Spirit descending from heaven like dove, and it remained on him. I myself did not know him, but the one who sent me to baptize with water said to me, 'He on whom you see the Spirit descend and remain is the one who baptizes with the Holy Spirit.' I myself have seen and have testified that this is the Son of God" (John 1:32-34).

Chapter Eleven

Christs Request from the Father

Christ requests from the Father that all Christian believers will be with Him in Heaven. The happiness of where Christ will consist of His presence; the very Heaven of Heaven is to be with Christ, to live with Him forever, to behold His glory, which the Father has given Him before the foundation of the world. "The glory of redeemer is the brightness of heaven. The Lamb is the light of the new Jerusalem" (Revelation 21:23). Jesus Christ knew the Father as no one has known the Father, therefore, in His priestly prayer, He approaches God, His Father with great confidence, as we react to people that we have known for a long time. Christ had known the Father. He is the mediator of a New Covenant. We are unworthy, Christ is worthy of all our praises. Jesus Christ prayed to the Father that the Spirit of love which filled Jesus Christ may fill all the believers, also, that a divine light should shine into their minds, a divine love may pour abroad into their hearts, to the point that they will partake in a divine nature. The love of God is through Jesus Christ our Lord; we must keep ourselves abiding in Christ, Christ in us, our hope of glory. Let all the believers keep their union in Christ and rejoice in His prayer of intercession for all our needs from the Father. All the believing Christians must praise our Lord Jesus Christ for His Priestly prayer for us before he left the Earth, and we should continue our prayer to Him, as He lives to make intercession for us, the prayer that can never be uttered. All the denominational churches in the world must read this prayer of our Lord again, and again and make sure they follow the unity, the union with Christ and make all their worship to be the same as other churches, be one in Him as he and the Father are one. Let all the churches keep the bond of unity in the perfect peace. Whatever is not in the Holy Bible should not be implemented. They have to remember that the Scripture said: do not add, or take away from this word of the Holy Bible, but people or some churches still add and take away on their own, to their congregation. Some of them denounce the important word of the gospel of God, such as the Cross, baptism and speaking in tongues.

"Nicodemus said to him, how can these things be? Jesus answered him, are you a teacher of Israel, and yet you do not understand these things (John 3: 9-10). Those who accept Jesus as Messiah experience the baptism of fire and judgment. The early church practice baptism, of imitation of the Lord Jesus Christ. There is also baptism of intimately related to faith in God, the baptism which identifies believers with the death and resurrection of Jesus Christ. Baptism also incorporates nonbelievers into the community of believers.

"Therefore, prepare your minds for action; be self-controlled; set your hope fully on the grace to be given you when Jesus Christ is revealed. As obedient children, do not conform to the evil desires you had when you lived in ignorance. But just as he who called you is holy, so be holy in all you do; for it is written: Be holy, because I am holy" *(1st Peter 1:13-16).*

Chapter Twelve

Our Lord's Final Prayer

Our Lord Jesus Christ's final prayer for His Disciples shows His deepest love, yearning for those who believe in Him during His early ministry and now. It shows a Spirit inspired example for all the servants of the Lord; how they should pray for all their congregation and value them when they gather together as one body of Christ and as children of God. They must pray for those who are under their care, their greatest concerns should be the believers may know Jesus Christ and His word intimately, they may see that God may keep them from the world, from temptations that cause them from falling away and to guard them from Satan and from false teacher's teachings. Believers may constantly possess the full joy of Christ in their lives, be holy in thought, in deed and in their characteristics and behavior. Believers may be one in their purposes and fellowship, as demonstrated by Christ Himself and the Father in so much that they may lead others to Christ, persevere in the faith and finally be able to be with Christ Jesus in Heaven. The love that the Father has for Christ may be in the believers, so much that they will love Jesus Christ with the same fervent love that the Father does, and that Christ by His Spirit may dwell in and with believers. Eternal life is more than endless existence; it is a special quality of life that believers receive when we partake of the essential life of God through Christ, which allows believers to know God the Father in an ever growing knowledge, relationship and fellowship with the Father, Son and Holy Spirit. Eternal life which presents the possession of life living by faith; it is secured and maintained by an activity of repentance and faith as it involves a present living union and living in fellowship.

Jesus Christ is the rock, the central figure from the Old Testament. He is the fore shadow and New Testament proclaims as prophecy become fact, Christ is the Messiah whom God anointed to redeem the people of the world. "Then he said to them, Hoh, how foolish you are, and how slow of heart to believe all that the prophets have declared! Was it not necessary that the Messiah should suffer these things and enter into his glory, Then beginning with Moses and all the prophets, he interpreted to them the things about himself in all the Scriptures" (Luke 24:25-27).

Chapter Thirteen

Eternal Life in Christ

Eternal life is associated with the believers' future hope of the coming of Christ for His faithful followers and it is combined with the believers' living by faith and by the Spirit of Holiness. Our Lord Jesus Christ's prayer for believers' protection, joy, sanctification, love and unity applies only to a particular people, to those who belong to God, to those who believe in Christ Jesus; to those who have consecrated themselves from the world and obey the Word of Jesus and accepted His teaching of the Gospel of God. Jesus Christ prayed to sanctify them, which means that God the Father should make them holy and separate, or set them apart. The evening before Christ's crucifixion, He prayed that His disciples will be a holy people, consecrated from the world and sin for the purpose of worshiping and serving the Lord. They must be set apart in order to be able to come near to God, and to be able to live for Him and to be like Him. Our Lord said: "Imitate me as I imitated my Father and do what is pleasing in his sight at all time" (John 8:29).   Sanctification could only be accomplished by believer' devotion to the truth revealed to them by the Holy Spirit of truth. The truth is the living Word of God and the revelation of God's written Word. Jesus Christ sanctifies Himself by setting Himself apart in order to do the will of His Father; means to die on the Cross. Jesus Christ suffered on the Cross in order that those who believe in Him might be separated from the world of sin and set themselves apart to the will of God the Father.

Christ also prayed for unity, which is spiritual unity based on living in Christ, knowing and experiencing the love of the Father and the fellowship of Jesus Christ. Separation from the world and sanctification in truth; receiving and believing the truth of the Word; obedience to the Word of the Father and the heart desire to bring salvation to the lost if any one of these factors are not, is missing; the true unity that Jesus prayed for cannot exist. Our Lord Jesus did not pray for His disciples and followers to become one, but rather that they may be one. The word used here designates ongoing actions of all believers.

They must continually be one in Christ as Christ is one with the Father. A oneness based on their common relationship to the Father and to the Son, and on having the same basic attitude towards the world, the Word and the need to reach out to the sinners and the lost. Attempt to create an artificial or fake unity by meetings, conferences, or complex organizations can result in a betrayal of the very unity for which Jesus prayed. What Jesus had in mind is much more than cosmetic unity meetings. It is a spiritual unity of heart, purpose; mind and will in those who are fully devoted to Christ, the Word, and holiness. Jesus Christ prayed that the glory that the Father gave Him, Christ was His life of self-denying service and His dying on the Cross in order to redeem the human race. Likewise, the glory of the believers is the path of humble service and bearing his or her cross. Humility, self-denial and the willingness to suffer for Christ will ensure the true unity of believers and it will lead to the true glory.

Though with a scornful wonder we see her sore oppressed by schisms rent asunder, by heresies distressed yet saints their watch are keeping, their cry goes up, how long? And soon the night of weeping shall be the morn of song. Mid toil and tribulation, and tumult of her war, she waits the consummation of peace forever more till with the vision glorious her longing eyes are blest and the great Church victorious shall be the Church at rest.

(Words Samuel J. Stone. 1866)

Chapter Fourteen

Jesus Christ - Our Great Intercessor

Intercession is defined as holy believing, persevering in prayer for oneself or where by a believer prayed and pleads with God on behalf of another believer who is desperately in need of God's intervention in their life. In the Book of Daniel, Daniel prayed earnestly for the restoration of Jerusalem as well as for the entire nation. The Scripture revealed that our Lord Jesus Christ made prayer of intercession with the Holy Spirit, also prayer of intercession is evident from the beginning of the Old Testament to the New Testament, in which men and women of God continue in up till this present day age. The intercession of Christ and the Holy Spirit during the early ministry of our Lord Jesus Christ was that He prayed for the sinners the lost that He came to the world to save. "For the Son of man came to seek and to save what was lost (Luke 19:10). Christ's earthly mission, the center of His heart and the core central of His mission on Earth is to save the sinners and the lost.

Jesus Christ wept over Jerusalem. He prayed for His disciples corporately and individually as a group. Christ prayed for His enemies when He was on the Cross. Scripture revealed also what Jesus said to Peter: "But I have prayed for you, Simon that your faith may not fail. And when you have turned back, strengthen your brothers" In another Scripture: " I tell you Peter, before the rooster crows today, you will deny three times that you know me" (Luke 22:32,34). The aspect of Christ's earthly ministry is to intercede on our behalf before God the Father's throne; "Who is he that condemns?" Christ Jesus, who died more than that, who was raised to life - is at the right hand of God and is also interceding for us"(Romans 8:34). "Therefore, he is able to save completely those who come to God through him, because he always lives to intercede for them" (Hebrews 7:25). Jesus Christ lives in Heaven in His Father's presence at the Father's right hand, interceding for each and every believing Christian according to the Father's will.

Through Jesus Christ's ministry of intercession, believers experience God's life and God's presence, and they find mercy and grace to help them in times of need. Temptations, weakness, sin and trial cannot prevail on the children of God because of Christ's High Priestly prayers for His people. His desire to pour out the Holy Spirit on all believers opens our heart to understand the content of Christ's intercessory ministry. "For we do not have a high priest who is unable to sympathize with our weakness but we have one who has been tempted in every way, just we are - yet was without sin"(Hebrews 4:15). "He is able to deal gently with those who are ignorant and are going astray, just as we are - yet was without sin" (Hebrews 4:15). "He is able to deal gently with those who are ignorant and are going astray, since he himself is subject to weakness" (Hebrew 5:2). "My dear children, I write this to you so that you will not sin, but if anybody does sin, we have one who speaks to the Father in our defense - Jesus Christ, the righteous one" (1st John 2:1). Apostle John believed that many born again believing Christians were still subject to sinning. However, he does not teach that Christians must sin, but instead he exhorts his believing Christians who will read the book to live without sin. Because those who willfully fall into sin, the care is that they confess and forsake that sin, in Jesus' death and resurrection as atoning sacrifice for our sins past, present and future sins. Christ's heavenly ministry is that He is the one who speaks to God the Father on our behalf and in our defense, He is our advocate; He is the foundation for our assurance of forgiveness and cleansing from sin, initially and continually.

Jesus Christ our Lord intercedes before God on our behalf on the basis of His atoning death and our active faith in Him, the one who believes in Him. Jesus Christ's intercession is very essential to believers' salvation. The Scripture has revealed: "Therefore, I will give him a portion among the great, and he will divide the spoil with the strong, because he poured out his life unto death, and was numbered with the transgressor. For he bore the sin of many, and made intercession for the transgressors" (Isaiah 53:12). God the Father promised to reward Jesus Christ for His atoning death, and Christ in turn promises to share His reward with all those who have strong faith, who follow Him in doing battle against sin and Satan through the power of the Holy Spirit. Christ's death on the Cross is a great inheritance, which has been released to God's children.

Any Gospel proclamation church that does not preach the cross of Christ and its deliverance from the power of sin is ultimately doomed to failure on this Earth; all such efforts will be empty of the presence of Jesus Christ and His Spirit. In Christ's agony on the Cross, Christ Jesus, our Lord and Savior, interceded for sinners. His ministry of intercession still continues in Heaven above at the right hand of the Father where He is seated. Without the grace, mercy and intercession, believers would have fallen away from God and once again became enslaved to sin.

The Holy Spirit is also involved in the ministry of intercession. "We do not know what we ought to pray for, but the Spirit himself intercedes for us with groans that words cannot express. And he who searches our hearts knows the mind of the Spirit, because the Spirit intercedes for the Saints in accordance with God's will" (Romans 8:26-27). The Holy Spirit's activities, including helping the believing Christians in prayer, all the children of God have two divine intercessors: Christ intercedes for the believers in Heaven and the Holy Spirit intercedes within the believers on Earth, "with groans" which pointed to the Spirit's intercession and travail within the believer and uttered by the believer. Our spiritual desires and yearnings as believers of Jesus Christ find their sources in the Holy Spirit, who dwells within us.

The Spirit himself sighs, groans and travails within us, longing for the day of our final redemption. He appeals to the Father on behalf of our needs in accordance with God the Father's will. The Scripture reveals that the believers' intercessory prayers, powerful prayers beginning from the Old Testament, the people, prophets and priests. An example of Old Testament intercession was Abraham's prayers for Ishmael: "And Elijah said to Ahab go, eat and drink, for there is the sound of a heavy rain. So Ahab went off to eat and drank, but Elijah climbed to the ground and put his face between his knees. Go and look towards the sea, he told his servant. And he went up and looked there is nothing there, he said. Seven times Elijah said, Go back. The seventh time the servant reported a cloud as small as a man's hand is rising from the sea. So Elijah said go and tell Ahab, hitch up your chariot and go down before the rain stops you. Meanwhile, the sky grew black with clouds, the wind rose, a heavy rain came on and Ahab rode off to Jezreel. The power of the Lord came upon Elijah and, tucking his cloak into his belt, he ran ahead of Ahab all the way to Jezreel" (1st King 18:41-46).

Elijah's faith filled and persistent prayer can be seen as an encouragement to all God's faithful people with regard to the power of prayer. Elijah's prayer was the prayer of a righteous man, the prayer of a man with a human nature like ours, an earnest and persistent prayer of faith, a prayer that accomplishes and avails much. The number seven in the Biblical Scripture symbolizes the full completion, whereby Elijah engaged in a complete intercession with three reasons. Elijah interceded to restore the alter and the honor of God in the land of Israel. He interceded by engaging in a spiritual warfare against false prophets' religion and the worshiping of Idols of Baalism that was spreading around the nation. He also interceded with God by intense and persistent prayers for the outpouring of rain in the land. Compared with the outpouring of the Holy Spirit in the Book of Joel 2:23-28 and in the Book of Acts 2:11.

Elijah's confrontation with the Idol worshipers of Baal illustrated the three main kinds of his intercession that must be characterized as the prayers of God's children as intercessory prayer revival that restores God's honor and glory among His people. Intercession and prayers that involved spiritual warfare against demonic strongholds of the enemy; intercession for spiritual drought to be broken by the outpouring of the Spirit of God and by spiritual awakening of the spirit, soul and body of believing Christians.

Daniel's intercessory of prayer: "So I turned to the Lord God and pleaded with him in prayer and petition, in fasting, and in sack cloth and ashes. I prayed to the Lord my God and confessed" (Daniel 9:3-4). Daniel understood that there are certain things that God has sovereignty appointed to come to pass at a certain time in the history of the world. Daniel prayed for the restoration of the Jewish captives in Babylon and Persia back to their home land was one such sovereign appointment of God; whereby many prophets spoke for example, Prophet Jeremiah; but there is also human responsibility in relation to what God has initiated, or what God has ordained. God therefore, calls intercessor to fast and travail in prayer for what he has appointed according to the Book of Daniel. Seventy years Jeremiah prophesied the restoration of Jerusalem and still there was no indication of the promised of the return and restoration. Therefore, Daniel was troubled in his heart; Daniel was expecting the fulfillment of Jeremiah's prophecy.

Daniel did not take it lightly or sit back waiting anymore, instead, he began to interceded; he plead earnestly in prayer and fasting for the fulfillment of God's Word. Daniel began his intercessory prayer by recognizing God's inspiring greatness, His faithfulness, His love and His covenant, His mercy that has been shown to those who love and obey Him. He made a confession identifying himself with the people of Israel who had sinned and rebelled against God. Daniel asked for Jerusalem's restoration not because of any righteousness on the part of Daniel or the nation of Israel, but for the Lord's sake; when God responded, He demonstrated His great mercy and loving compassion as a God who fulfills His promises.

We see Moses life in the Old Testament as an example of powerful prayer of intercession. On many occasions Moses prayed intensely to God to change His declared intention, even when God had told Moses His reason for His action. When the Israelites rebelled against God in the wilderness, Moses prayed and pleaded for the children of Israel and God answered Moses prayers, letting him know that he has forgiven the Israelites according to Moses' prayer.

In the New Testament Scripture it is revealed how parents and other people and friends interceded for their loved one and pleaded to Christ for healing. "Then one of the synagogue rulers, named Jairus came there seeing

Jesus, he fell at his feet and pleaded earnestly with him my little daughter is dying please come and put your hands on her so that she will be healed and live so Jesus went with him" (Mark 5:22-24). We see here the example of parent pleading for his child so that Jesus might come and heal him. "Now Jesus himself had pointed out that a prophet has no honor in his own country" (John 4: 43, 47). When this man heard that Jesus had arrived in Galilee from Judea, he went to him and begged him to come and heal his son, who was close to death." "People were bringing little children to Jesus to have him touch them but the disciples rebuked them.

When Jesus saw this, he was indignant. He said to them, let the little children come to me, and do not hinder them, for the kingdom of God belongs to such as these. I tell you the truth; anyone who will not receive the kingdom of God like a little child will never enter it. And he took the children in his arms, put his hands on them and blessed them" (Mark 10: 13-16). The Kingdom and receiving the Kingdom of God like a child means accepting the Kingdom of God in a simple, humble, trustful, faithful and wholehearted behavior, to turn from sin like a little child who listens to his or her parents, receiving Christ Jesus as your personal Lord and Savior, and God as your heavenly

Father whom only you go to in everything that you are going through on this Earth.

Jesus Christ very, very concerned about the salvation of all the people in the world and the spiritual upbringing of children, parents must train, educat their children about God. Christian believing parents must use every means, making all efforts of the grace of God that is available to bring their children to Jesus Christ, for our Lord and Savor longs to receive them, love them and bless them. We see a man pleaded for his servant to be healed and the mother of James and John, interceded with Jesus on their behalf.

Many local churches interceded on behalf of various individual problems in the church. For example, the early church in Jerusalem gathered together and offered prayer of intercession for Peter while he was in prison and Peter was released by angels (Acts 12:5, 12). In Antioch the church offered prayer of intercession on behalf of Apostle Paul and Barnabas (Act 13:3). James' instruction during the time of early church in Jerusalem was that the elders of the church must pray for the sick and for all Christians to pray for each other. Apostle Paul urges every believer to pray for everyone, while we see Paul himself as a prayer warrior. Paul interceded for all the churches of

God everywhere. Also, Paul always asked the church to pray for him in everything he was going through then so that his ministry may be empowered and move forward with Christ's fullness. In the numerous intercessory prayers of the Scripture, people of God pleaded with God to bless His people, to deliver them from temptation, danger, affliction and persecution in various forms. It also includes the Holy Spirit intercessor's prayer in the life of all those who believe in Jesus and for the Spirit empowerment to be bestowed on all individual Christians. As well as for the power of healing to those who are sick, distressed and the weak with the prayer of the Holy Spirit for the forgiveness of sins, coupled with the ability of the people of God and authority of the Word of God, to rule the heart. The believing Christians' may grow in grace and in supplications. The intercessory prayers of our Lord and Savior manifest continuously; calling the laborers into the harvest field according to His will. For missionary work in the world to continue to grow and expand, flooding the four corners of the Earth. The Holy Spirit prayer of an intercessor is for the salvation of all the people in the world. People of God open their mouth wide and praise God, the Father as well as reveals the will of God for His children.

All the Christian believers should focus appropriately on intercessory prayers, so that God will always be honored in the power of a persevering prayer of faith in their lives. The intercessory prayer that our Lord and Savior will continue to intercede for is the Saints on the Earth, for the Gospel to reach the unreachable in their own language, for He lives to intercede for those who loves Him.

When God the Spirit came upon his church outpoured in sound of wind and sign of flame they spread his truth abroad, and filled with the Spirit proclaimed that Christ is Lord. What courage, power and grace that youthful church displayed! To those of every tribe and race they witnessed unafraid, and filled with the Spirit they broke their bread and prayed.

(Words of Timothy Dudley –Smith, 1977)

Chapter Fifteen

Church Purpose

Church purpose is primarily is for people of God and its purpose is to worship God in Spirit and in truth, live a life that is pleasing in God's sight, and a life of love as God loves you and gave Himself for you. The Scripture reveals, "If your brother sins against you go and show him his fault, just between the two of you. If he listens to you, you have won your brother over, but if he will not listen, take one or two others along, so that every matter may be established by the testimony of two or three witnesses. If he refuses to listen to them, tell it to the church; and if he refuses to listen even to the church, treat him as you would a pagan or a tax collector" (Matthew 18:15-17). One of the important purpose of the church is to set the method of restoring or disciplining a professing Christian who sins against another member of the church in a private manner. Neglecting Christ's instruction will bring spiritual compromise and eternal consequences to the church as a holy people of God. The purpose of the church discipline is to protect God's dignity and reputation, to guard the moral purity and the doctrinal integrity of the church and to attempt to save way ward members and restore them to full Christ likeness. "When they came to Jerusalem, they were welcome by the church and the apostles and the elders, to whom they reported everything that God had done through them" (Acts 15:4). The main purpose of the church is to make disciples of all the people in all the nations to know God, give their life to God through our Lord Jesus Christ. The purpose is to let the people of this Earth know that God is love and He sent His only begotten Son, Jesus Christ, to this world; to save the sinners and the lost.

*They saw God's Word prevail, His kingdom still increase,
no part of all His purpose fail, no promised blessing cease,
and filled with the Spirit knew love and joy and peace.
Their theme was Christ alone, the Lord who lived and died,
who rose to His eternal throne at God the Father's side;
and filled with the Spirit the church was multiplied.
(Words of Timothy Dudley-smith, 1977)*

Chapter Sixteen

The Universal Church of Christ

"The gates of Hades will not overcome it" (Matthew 16:18b).   Our Lord Jesus Christ was telling Apostle Peter that the gates of Hades will not over power the church He is going to build or the church He is building on this universe at that time and until His return. The gates of Hades mean or represented all the demons and evil strategy that Satan can marshal or put together in an attempt to destroy the Church or to withstand its mission in the Universe. This Scripture was not directed to Christian believers, local churches, fellowship of churches, or any denominational churches, they will never fall away in doctrinal errors, or otherwise be overcome by sin or the snares of Satan. Jesus Christ himself warned all the believing Christians and churches of possible spiritual deception and failure. Scripture revealed: "At that time many will turn away from the faith and will betray and hate each other, and many false prophets will appear and deceive many people. Because of the increase of wickedness, the love of most will grow cold, but he who stands firm to the end will be saved. And this gospel of the kingdom will be preached in the whole world as a testimony to all nations, and then the end will come" (Matthew 24:10-14). This gospel of the Kingdom will be preached and taught in so many ways, in everyone's language, every people in the world will have the Gospel preached, explained and analyzed to them in the language that they speak. This is when the end will come because our Lord Jesus Christ does not want anyone to perish; He wants them to come to the knowledge of repentance and prayer for the forgiveness of sin, which is only in Him. Only after the gospel of the Kingdom has been adequately preached in the whole world, will the end come. The Gospel will be preached taught in the power and righteousness of the Holy Spirit, that will be accompanied by major signs of the Gospel. Only Jesus Christ and God the Father will know when this task is accomplished according to His purpose.

The Christian believers' task is to faithfully and continuously press on to all the nations till our Lord returns to take His church to Heaven. According to the Scripture: "Then Jesus came to them and said all authority in heaven and on earth has been given to me. Therefore, go and make disciples of all nations, baptizing them in the name of the Father and of the Son and of the Holy Spirit, and teaching them to obey everything I have commanded you and surely I am with you always to the very end of the age" (Matthew 28:18-20). Our Lord Jesus Christ gave the apostles and all His followers before He ascended to Heaven the Great Commission with the word of authority. He said all authority has been given to Him, not to anyone else; this is His word of assurance that God's people must always be standing on in this world. Christ has all authority in Heaven and on Earth. God's people (all the Christian believers) are promised authority and power to proclaim the Gospel throughout the world.

But first they must obey Jesus' commandment to wait for the promise of the Father, which is the power of the Holy Spirit Pentecost. The Holy Spirit is the power source of Christians in the world. Believers cannot expect the power of the baptism in the Holy Spirit to impart power to preach Jesus as Lord and Savior. He will also increase the effectiveness of our witness, strengthen and deepen our relationship with God the Father, Son and Holy Spirit, which comes from being filled with the Holy Spirit. The power of the Holy Spirit is the one that will accompany the believers in an ongoing of the service of the Lord. The command of the Lord can only be accomplished by the power and the presence of the indwelling of the Holy Spirit. The Holy Spirit will accompany the missionaries, the pastors, ministers of the Word of God going to all the nations and they will also follow the pattern of the Holy Spirit.

The words of Jesus Christ concerning the Great Commission to all His disciples and all the believers from generation to generation is the standard and remains forever. Christ's goal is to see all the believing Christians - the Church as the universal church, local church, house church that were commissioned by the Lord, as they were given responsibility to take the Gospel to the end of the world. All the believers must know clearly that the preaching of the Gospel is centered primarily on repentance and forgiveness of sins. The purpose is to make disciples, not just converts, who will observe Christ's commands. Christ does not intend that evangelism and missionary witness result only in conversion. Spiritual energies must not be concentrated in enlarging church membership, increasing the number of the congregation, but focus also on making disciples.

Disciples are those Christians who separated themselves from the world, observe the commands of Christ, and follow Him with all their heart, mind and will. Scripture revealed: "…to the Jews who had believed him, Jesus said: If you hold to my teaching, you are really my disciples. Then you will know the truth and the truth will set you free" (John 8:31-32). Jesus Christ was telling the people during His earthly ministry to hold on to His teaching, to listen to His teaching, to learn from His teaching, to take His teaching seriously by taking it to their heart. Christ did not encourage His Disciples to place their confidence on past faith, or past experience. He was lecturing them that it is only when they hold to His teaching that the confidence of salvation will be open to them. The true and genuine disciples of Christ will continue to obey the words of Jesus. Christ Our Lord said that the truth will set all His disciples, and all the believers free. In view of human knowledge, there are many things that are true and there are many things that are not true. Therefore, there is only one truth that will set people free from sin, death, destruction and Satan's dominion; it is the truth of Jesus Christ Himself and His revelation of truth in the Scripture. There are three important observations about the truth - Scripture, especially the original revelation of Jesus Christ from the beginning of the New Testament and the apostles, testimony, which testifies to the truth that frees one from sin, the world and the demonic power.

The revelation of the truth is not needed to complete or make more adequate for the gospel of Christ. Saving truth that is revealed only from God the Father by the Holy Spirit, which does not originate from any human being, or from any humanistic wisdom. We have to remember at all times that Christ commands us to concentrate on reaching to lost sinners, the lost men, women and children that are not in a Christian society that is not spreading the Gospel to the world. Those who believe must come out of the current evil world system and be separated from its immorality.

Those who believe in Christ and in the gospel of God are to be baptized in order to renounce all immorality, the world and their own sinful nature, and to truthfully commit themselves to Christ and His Kingdom purposes. Jesus Christ will always be with His obedient believers in the presence and in the power of the Holy Spirit. They are to go to all the nations and witness after they have been clothed with the power from above. Our Lord and Savior

Jesus Christ promises that He will be with His people in the presence of the Holy Spirit and His authority would be with all the Christian believers who go forth to make disciples among all the people in the world.

Jesus Christ is presently with us in the person of the Holy Spirit and through His Word. No matter what condition, what problems: weak, poor, humble, rich, someone who is unimportant, Christ cares for you, watches over you and is concerned with every detail of your life's trials and struggles, and gives you His grace that is sufficient and His presence to lead you home. This is the Christian's answer to every fear, every doubt, every trouble, every heartache and every discouragement.

O good Jesus, the Word of the Father, the brightness of Father's glory, who angels desire to behold: Teach me to do your will – that guided by your good spirit, I may come unto that blessed city where there is everlasting day and all are of one spirit; where there is certain security and secure eternity, and eternal tranquility and quiet felicity, and happy sweetness and sweet pleasantness; where you, with the Father and the Holy Spirit, live and reign, world without end. Amen

(Words of Gregory the Great 7th century)

Chapter Seventeen

Christ: the Head of the Church

"To the church of God in Corinth, to those sanctified in Christ Jesus and called to be Holy together with all those everywhere who call on the name of our Lord Jesus Christ their Lord and ours" (1st Corinthians 1:2). The Scripture revealed that our Lord sent Ananias to Paul during his conversion, or encounter with our Lord Jesus Christ on the road to Damascus, but Ananias answered the Lord. "Lord," Ananias answered, 'I have heard many reports about this man and all the harm he has done to your saints in Jerusalem. And he has come here with authority from the chief priests to arrest all who call on your name" (Acts 9: 13-14). After Paul encounters Jesus Christ on the road to Damascus, and accepted Him as Lord and the Messiah who is to come, he fasts and prays for guidance with an attitude of deep commitment to God. All the believers must realize that a saving encounter with Christ Jesus should always result in a spiritual hunger and longing to know Jesus, and to follow His footsteps, His commandments and His teaching. The early church believers were called Saints – this refers to the people that were separated from sin and to God. Saints consecrated themselves from the world, that means they are being led and sanctified by the Holy Spirit and have fully committed their lives to Jesus Christ. Calling believers Saints does not mean they are perfect, or incapable of committing sin. It is a common Biblical name for the believers that emphasizes the Scriptures and the scriptural expectation that all the believers were conformed to the way of God's righteousness and the necessity that says holiness is the way; this must be an eternal reality for all who belong to Christ.

Therefore, the Scriptures reveal, "It is because of him that you are in Christ Jesus who has become for us wisdom from God - that is, our righteousness, holiness and redemption. Therefore, as it is written, let him who boasts, boast in the Lord" (1st Corinthians 1:30-31). Jesus Christ, the head of the Church, has become for us wisdom. It is through Christ, in Christ and with Christ, that all the believing Christians receive wisdom from God and experience the righteousness of God, the sanctification and redemption. "But now righteousness from God, apart from the Law, has been made known, to which the Law and the Prophets testify. This righteousness from God comes through faith in Jesus Christ to all who believe. There is no difference, for all have sinned and fall short of the glory of God, and are justified freely by his grace through the redemption that came by Jesus Christ" (Romans 3:21-24). As long as we joined in unity with Christ, Christ Jesus is the source of all these blessings. The sinfulness of everyone on this Earth shows that they were in need of the gospel of God. The Good News of the gospel of God's grace is forgiveness and redemption in Christ our Lord. Righteousness from God refers to God's redemptive activity in the life of human's sins, by which Christ is the justifier, of who have faith in Him, and put the sinner who repent and receive forgiveness in the right relationship with Himself as well as liberated believers from the power of evil. The working of God's grace of salvation and the manifestation of His righteousness are very essential for believers.

This revelation of God's righteousness in the Gospel is not something that ended; it is an ongoing until we leave this world. Because the power of God for salvation that accompanies every believer, is constantly refreshes and it is relevant in the life of every Christian. The righteousness of God comes to the believers as a free gift through faith in Jesus Christ. Faith in Jesus Christ as our Lord and Savior is the one and only condition that God the Father requires for salvation. Jesus Christ is the head of the Church through His atoning sacrifice, an offering of His blood and His life for sinners on the Cross. Christ died not for His own sake, but for the sake of all the people in the world. Christ's substitutional sacrifice, as He suffered death as the penalty for your and mine sins, and for the sins of every human race. Christ is the believers' substitute; He is the head of the Church. We have to look at Christ's death as a propitiatory for sinners. Christ's death for sinners satisfied God's righteous nature and His moral order, where God removed His wrath despite anything they do.

Therefore, Christ's likeness should be the first and the foremost for all that includes love for God and love for other people in the world. The believers' love for God will motivate, structure them, shape them, and move them to have love for every people in the world. Just as Christ's love for God was always first and His love for others subordinate to and based on that love for the Father.

Christ's love for His Father was revealed in His concern for God's glory, for God's will, for God's Word and God's nearness of His presence. We see Jesus' love for the Father in His faithfulness to God and in His willingness to carry out God's will by sacrificing His life for our redemption.

Finally Christ's love for His Father is further revealed in His love for righteousness and hatred of sin. Christ's love for humanity was seen in His compassion, kindness, humility, gentleness and patience. Christ also demonstrated His love by rebuking sin in the lives of all people in the world. Christ's love to humanity expressed His anger at those who were cruel, heartless, or insensitive to the suffering and the needs of others. He warned us of Hell and offered Himself as an atoning sacrifice for our sin.

Christ whose glory fills the skies, Christ, the true the only light, Sun of righteousness, arise, triumph over shades of night. Day spring from on high, be near, Daystar, in my heart appear! Dark and cheerless is the dawn till your glories shine on me; joyless is the day's return till your mercy's beams I see; as they inward light import, cheer my eyes and warm my heart.

(Words of Charles Wesley, 1740)

Chapter Eighteen

Christ: the Church Cornerstone

"Who have been chosen according to the foreknowledge of God the Father, through the sanctifying work of the Spirit, for obedience to Jesus? Christ and sprinkling by his blood. grace and peace be yours in abundance." (1st Peter 1:2). The people of God are chosen to be God's people according to His foreknowledge of His plan of redemption and according to God's one comprehensive knowledge of His plan of redemption in Christ for the Church, even before creation and before the human history began. "For those he foreknew, he also predestinated to be conformed to the likeness of his Son, that he might be the first born among many brothers" (Roman 8:29). This Scripture is telling us that those He foreknew means He beforehand loved and chose to bestow love to choose to love a person from Earth to eternity. Foreknowledge means that God purposed from eternity to love and redeem the human race through Jesus Christ. It also means that the recipient of God's foreknowledge or fore love is stated in the plural refers to the church, the body of Christ. Which means that God's fore love is primarily for the corporate body of Jesus Christ, and it includes the individuals, only as they identify themselves with Christ's corporate body through the abiding faith in and through union with Christ.

The corporate body of Christ will attain to glorification; individual of believers may fall short of the glorification if they separate themselves from that fore loved body and fail to maintain their faith in Christ. The person of Christ is central to this righteousness, for by Jesus Christ and only by Him, God has worked in a truly indescribable way to save human beings to reconcile them to Himself, to bring them out of the bondage of sin, out of desperation and despair into hope in Him, and out of death to life. What humanity cannot do for themselves because of their sinfulness and weakness, the God of mercy did it for them through the redemptive work of Jesus Christ's life and death and resurrection. Believer's response to God's good news is faith, faith in Christ is an open admission that says we cannot earn God's approval by our own merit effort, but we must stretch out our empty hands in order to receive God's free offer of forgiveness, grace, and love, in Jesus Christ.

Faith is therefore our personality in the personal address of God in Jesus Christ. Jesus Christ built only one church; we all are one in Him, people of this world have turned around and built many churches according to their own choice and according to how they interpreted the Scriptures. Jesus Christ is the head of the church: "For the husband is the head of the wife as Christ is the head of the church, his body of which he is the Savior" (Ephesians 5:23). Jesus Christ is the only Savior - of His one body, which is the believers, and His one church. In his work of redemption, he only plans to have one body, one church and to save only one Church, which is his church.

Families

God has established the family as the basic unit in society. Every family must have a leader; therefore, God has assigned to the husband the responsibility of being the head of the wife and family. Christ's headship must be exercised in love, gentleness and consideration for his wife and family. The husband's God given responsibility as head of the wife includes: provision for the family's spiritual and domestic needs, love, protection and interest in her welfare in the same way that Christ loves the church; honor, and understanding, appreciation and thoughtfulness, are absolute faithfulness to the marriage relationship. The Scripture reveals that the same way we must see Christ as the head of the church, which the Lord God built. Jesus Christ promised to save His body, His church. "He replied every plant that my heavenly Father has not planted will be pulled up by the roots. Leave them: They are blind guides. If a blind man leads a blind man, both will fall into a pit" (Matthew 15: 13-14). God rooted up all the false prophets, all those who call unto Him, all those who are using His holy name for money they will be uprooted. The one church of Jesus Christ, which he purchased with His own precious blood, belongs to Him.

It is good and profitable the souls if people attend the church of God's choice, the church that Christ purchases with His own blood. To persevere in true faith, is to trust God in all circumstances and remain true to Him, even when you are in great trouble and He does not seem to answer or it seems that He does not care. Christ is testing our faith when we experience this type of silence from Christ. The Scripture reveals: "Unless the Lord builds the house, its builders labor in vain, unless the Lord watches over the city, the watchman stand guard in vain" (Psalm 127:1). All the servants of the Lord, all the believers, who labored to build God's house on Earth, they must make sure that they built it according to His pattern and by His Spirit, not according to human power, or ideas, plans and efforts.

"Greet one another with a holy kiss. All churches of Christ send greetings" (Romans 16:16-17). In Paul's last letter, he gives a strong warning to the church in Rome to be alert of all those who do damage to the church of Christ by corrupting the teaching of Paul and the other apostles. They are to watch out for the proponents of false doctrine and reject and stay away from them and from their ministry. The name of the church of Christ glorifies and honors to Jesus Christ, the one and only who built the Church. Apostle Paul preaches and teaches about unity in the church, it was badly received and not achieved because the church split into two groups during the early church era. Hebrew converts and the Gentile converts. The unity was never achieved. The moment we give our life to Jesus Christ, we are automatically placing our spirit, soul and body in the body of Christ who is the head of the church. This is the reason why the scripture says: Therefore, if anyone is in Christ, he is a new creation, old things have passed away; behold, all things have become new " (2nd Corinthians 5:17). Through the creative commandment of God, those who accept Jesus Christ by faith are made a new creation; that means they belongs totally to God's new world in which the Spirit of God rules. The believer will become a new person; renewed after God's image. Sharing God's glory with a renewed knowledge and understanding, wisdom and the new believers will be living a life of holiness.

The Scripture continues to help our understanding and says: "But as many as receive him, to them gave the power to become the Sons of God, even to them that believe on his name. Which was born, not of blood, nor of the will of the flesh, nor of the will of man, but of God (John 1:12-13). Yet to all who received Him, to those which believed in His name, He gave the right to become children of God children born not of natural descent, nor human decision or a husband's will but born of God. These two verses in the Book of John states clearly how saving faith is both the actions of a single instant and an ongoing attitude of a lifetime. To become a child of God, we must receive Christ by faith. Following the sinner's action of faith, there must be continual actions of believing in a believer. The word believed is a present participle, which describe a continued action on behalf of the believer and indicating the need for perseverance in believing. In order for one to be finally saved, true faith must continue after the initial action of accepting Jesus Christ. It is very important to know that Apostle John never uses "belief." Yet, he uses "believe" because John knows that saving faith is an activity; something that people can do. True faith is not static belief and trust in Christ Jesus and His redemptive work. But a loving, self - abandoning commitment that constantly draws one near and nearer to our Lord and Savior Jesus Christ in spiritual intimacy. As children of God we have the right to become the adopted children of God only if they believe in the name of Christ when they receive Christ, they are born again and become God's children; not all the people on Earth are God's children.

Visit then this soul of mine, pierce the gloom of sin and grief; fill me, radiancy divine, scatter all my unbelief; more and more yourself display, shining to the perfect day! You are good, our God, and you are good to us. You have spoken the word of creation, redemption, and guidance, and have given us life.

(Words of Charles Wesley 1740)

Chapter Nineteen

The Church Is a Spiritual Fellowship

"If you then, though you are evil, know how to give good gifts to your children, how much more will your Father in heaven give the Holy Spirit to those who ask him" (Luke 11:13). This verse refers to the impartation of the Spirit at the new birth. From the moment at conversion all believers are automatically given the indwelling presence of the Holy Spirit. Our Lord and Savior said: "In reply Jesus declared, 'I tell you the truth, on one can see the kingdom of God unless he is born again" (John 3:3). The Lord Jesus Christ teaches that without the new birth no one can see the Kingdom of God, and receive eternal life and salvation through Jesus Christ. The foundational doctrine of all the believing Christians' faith is based on spiritual birth, or what the Scripture called regeneration. The fact is that regeneration means a recreating of spiritual life in the human heart by God the Holy Spirit. Through this process, eternal life from God Himself is imparted to the believer's heart. The Scripture revealed, " For God so loved the world that he gave his one and only Son, that whoever believes in him shall not perish but have eternal life" (John 3:16). The verse reveals the heart and purpose of God towards humanity. God's love is so wide enough to embrace all the people in the world. God gave His one and only begotten Son as an offering for Sin on the Cross. The atonement proceeds from the loving heart of God the Father Almighty. It was not something that was forced on Him.

Spiritual Church Fellowship

"May the grace of the Lord Jesus Christ, and the love of God and the fellowship of the Holy Spirit be with you all" (2nd Corinthians 13:14). Here we see clearly the New Testament church's belief, which is in the Trinity. The apostles pray and pray that the Corinthians church may continually experience the grace of Jesus Christ, His nearness, His power, and His comfort in their life. He prays that they will be able to experience the Fatherly love of God with all His blessings and a deepening fellowship with the Holy Spirit. If all the believing Christians in the world hold on to this threefold reality they will have the abiding blessings, and their everlasting salvation will be very sure as well as full of joy. Fellowship helps all the believers to demonstrate an observable love and care for one another.

The unity of the Spirit and the baptism in the Spirit, the Scripture says, "John Baptized with water but in a few days you will be baptized with the Holy Spirit" (Acts 1:5). The baptism in the Holy Spirit is intended for all who put their faith in Jesus Christ, and have been born again, as well as have received the indwelling of the Holy Spirit. The primary purpose of baptism in the Holy Spirit is the receiving of power to witness for Christ so that the lost will be won over to Him and taught to obey all that Christ commanded.

"Bless the Lord, O my soul, and all that is within me, bless his holy name. Bless the Lord, O my soul, and do not forget all his benefits who forgives all your iniquity, who heals all your diseases, who redeems your life from the Pit, who crowns you with steadfast love and mercy, who satisfies you with good as long as you live so that your youth is renewed like the eagle's" (Psalm 103).

Chapter Twenty

The Church: A Spiritual Ministry

The church as a spiritual ministry serves through the use of gifts bestowed by the Holy Spirit upon the believers. "We have different gifts, according to the grace, given us. If a man's gift is prophesying, let him use it in proportion to his faith. If it is serving, let him serve; If it is teaching let him teach" (Roman 12:6-7). The God the Holy Spirit gave gifts according to everyone's inward ability. The gift of grace full of inward desires or dispositions as well as enablement or abilities given by the Holy Spirit to individuals in the congregation to build up God's people and express God's love to others.

All the believing Christians have at least one gift of the Holy Spirit. However, believers primary gift does not exclude the exercise of any other gifts as need may arise.

Serving is the God given desire, ability and power to give practical assistance to members and leaders of the church helping them to fulfill their responsibility to God. Teaching is God's given desire, with the ability and power to examine and study God's Word, and to clarify, defend and proclaim the truth in such a way that other people of all other religions may grow in grace and in godliness. "Therefore, you do not lack any spiritual gift as you eagerly wait for our Lord Jesus Christ to be revealed" (1st Corinthians 1:7). All the believing Christians must wait for our Lord and Savior just as in early Christianity, they lived in expectation of Christ's imminent return. Believers fixed their faith firmly on the fact of the Lord's coming. They lived everyday in anticipation of that great hope. "And in the church God has appointed first of all apostles, second prophets, third teachers, then workers of miracles, also those having gifts of healing, those able to help others, those with gifts of administration, and those speaking in different kinds of tongues? Are all prophets? Are all teachers? Do all work miracles? Do all have gifts of healing? Do all speak in tongues? Do all do all interpret? But eagerly desire the greater gifts" (1st Corinthians 12:28-31). In the Church, God Almighty appointed several individuals and gave them the gift of the Holy Spirit that includes the manifestation of spiritual gifts as well as description of various gifts in the body of Christ. Most believers baptized in the Holy Spirit find it easy to pray in tongues as they yield themselves to the Spirit on the Day of Pentecost. All those who were filled with the Spirit spoke in tongues as a sign that they had received the fullness of the Holy Spirit.

The Scripture reveals in the spiritual ministry, "It was he who gave some to be apostles, some to be prophets, some to be evangelists, and some to be pastors and teachers" (Ephesians 4:11). Christ's gift of the Holy Spirit and spiritual gifts indicates that one of the foremost purposes for which Christ gives gifts to the leaders of the church is for them to train, equip and prepare the entire body of Christ to the work of ministry. Every member in the body of Christ, professional ministers do most of the ministry work. Every believing Christian must be trained and released for ministry in some sphere so that multiplication of edification and growth may be manifest in the Church according to the New Testament doctrine.

The Lord works vindication and justice for all who are oppressed. He made known his ways to Moses, his acts to the people of Israel. The Lord is merciful and gracious; slow to anger and abounding in steadfast love. He will not always accuse, nor will he keep his anger forever. He does not deal with us according to our sins, nor repay us according to our iniquities" (Psalm 103).

Chapter Twenty - One

The Church: An Army in Spiritual Conflict

The Church fights by the sword of the Spirit and always involves spiritual conflict. It fights by the sword and by the power of the Holy Spirit. Scripture says: "Take the helmet of salvation and the sword of the Spirit, which is the Word of God. And pray in the Spirit on all occasions with all kinds of prayers and requests. With this in mind, be alert and always keep on praying for all the Saints" (Ephesians 6:17-18). The sword of the Spirit is our offensive weapon in spiritual warfare in this world. Satan will make every effort to undermine or destroy our confidence in that sword, which is the Word of God.

The Church must defend the inspired Scriptures against allegations that Scripture is not God's Word in everything it teaches. To abandon the attitude of Jesus and the apostles toward God's inspired word is to destroy its power to rebuke or correct, to redeem, to heal, to drive out demons and to overcome all evil. To deny Scripture's absolute trust worthiness in all it teaches is to deliver ourselves into Satan's hand. Our warfare against Satan's spiritual forces calls for an intensity in prayer, praying in the Spirit for all the believers with continued prayer. Prayer must be seen as not just as another weapon, but must be seen as part of the actual conflict in itself, where the victory is won for ourselves and others by working together with God Himself. Failing to pray diligently, with all kinds of prayers in all situations, is to surrender to the enemy. The Church is in a spiritual struggle against Satan and sin.

The Spirit, with which the Church is filled, is like a warrior wielding the living Word of God, delivering people from Satan's dominion and conquering every power of this dark world. "To open their eyes and turn them from the power of Satan to God, so that they may receive forgiveness of sins and a place among those who are sanctified by faith in me" (Acts 26:18). This classic statement of the word of our Lord Jesus Christ was a divine commission given to Apostle Paul. What our Lord desires from the preaching of the Gospel to the sinners and the lost is to open the eyes of those people in this world that Satan blinds their eyes, especially the nonbelievers and unsaved that faced the reality of their lost and their perishing condition and turn to the truth of the Gospel.

The preaching teaching of Jesus Christ in the power of the Holy Spirit will open their minds to the understanding of the Scripture that will allow the Holy Spirit to reflect God's highest desire for every believer in Christ and prayer that the Spirit will work in them in a greater measure. The reason for the Holy Spirit increased measure of the Spirit's impartation is that believers may receive more wisdom, revelation and knowledge; not condemning God's work of redemptive purposes for the present and for the future salvation. And those believers may experience a more abundant power of the Holy Spirit in their lives.

Therefore, in order for believing Christians to advance in grace, achieve victory over Satan and sin, witness effectively for Jesus Christ and gain final salvation, God's Holy Spirit and power must be manifestly present with the believer. This power is activities of manifestation and strength of the Holy Spirit working within believers faithfully. The Spirit which filled the Church is like a warrior wielding the living Word of God that is delivering people of God from the dominion of Satan and conquering every power of darkness on this Earth.

The proclamation of the Gospel in the power of the Spirit will rescue men and women from the power of Satan as well as bring them into the Kingdom of Jesus Christ, that they may receive forgiveness of sins, forgiveness that comes through faith in Christ that is based primarily on Jesus' sacrificial death on the Cross. Everyone that repents and received forgiveness of their sins from Jesus Christ, and their sins are forgiven, they have been automatically delivered from the dominion of sin, death and Satan. They have also been baptized in the Holy Spirit, set apart from the world and they are now lives unto God in the fellowship with all the saved believing Christians who placed their faith in Christ Jesus.

The Scripture reveals, "Put on the full armor of God so that you can take your stand against the devil's schemes. For our struggle is not against flesh and blood, but against the rulers, against the spiritual forces of evil in the heavenly realms. Therefore, put on the full armor of God, so that when the day of evil comes, you may be able to stand your ground, and after you have done everything, to stand. Stand firm then, with the belt of truth, buckled around your waist, with the breastplate of righteousness in place, and with your feet fitted with the readiness that comes from the gospel of peace" (Ephesians 6:11-15). All the believing Christians in this world face a spiritual conflict with Satan and a host of evil spirits. This power of darkness in the world are the spiritual forces of evil which manifest in various forms and various ways which energize the ungodly and make them to oppose the will of God, and which also frequently attack those believers of Christ of the world, or on Earth. They are in great multitude and organized into an empire of evil with rank and order.

The Sword of the Spirit is our offensive weapon in any spiritual warfare. Satan will make, use, and take every effort to undermine or destroy our confidence in that Sword, which is the Word of God. The church must defend the inspired Scriptures against the allegations that say the Scriptures are not the Word of God in everything, it teaches. To abandon the attitude of Jesus and the apostles toward God's inspired Word is to knowingly destroy the power of the Scripture that correct, redeem, to heal, to drive our demons and to overcome all evil. To deny Scripture's absolute trustworthiness in all it teaches is to deliver ourselves into Satan's hand. Our warfare against Satan's spiritual forces calls for an intensity in prayer - we must be praying in the Spirit, at all times with all kinds of prayers for all the believers, we must continue praying, we must see prayer as part of the conflict itself, where victory is won for ourselves and for others by working together with our heavenly Father. Therefore, believers must make every effort to belong to Christ, not only to any denominational or to any group alone, they must make sure that they belong to Christ.

We are put in Jesus Christ to become a new creature in Him, not in a denominational church. Becoming part of an early assembly church is the natural outcome of the new birth after we have been saved. To be born again of the Spirit is to have the Spirit of Christ that indwells us and living his life through us from this Earth to Heaven. If anyone does not have the Spirit of Christ they are not fully converted. Born of God is to have the Holy Spirit lives inside the believer maintaining good relationship with God the Father, Son, and God the Holy Spirit - ever one God.

"*For as the heavens are high above the earth, so great is his steadfast love toward those who fear him; as far as the east is from the west, so far he removes our transgressions from us. As a father has compassion for his children, so the Lord has compassion for those who fear him. For he knows how we were made; he remembers that we are dust*" *(Psalm 103).*

Chapter Twenty-Two

The Church: the Pillar & Ground of Truth

"If I am delayed, you will know how people ought to conduct themselves in God's household, which is the church of the living God, the pillar and foundation of the truth" (1st Timothy 3:15). The Church must be the foundation of the truth of the gospel of God to the nations of Earth. The Church of Jesus Christ must uphold and preserve the truth revealed by Christ and the apostles by receiving and obeying it. The Scriptures says: "But the one who received the seed that fell on good soil is the man who hears the word and understands it. He produces a crop, yielding a hundred, sixty or thirty times what was sown" (Matthew 13:23). The parable of our Lord and Savior of the wheat and weeds emphasizes that Satan will sow alongside those who sow the Word of God which the field represents the world or the Universe. The good seed represents the true believing Christians, Sons and daughters of the Kingdom. The Gospel and the true believers will be planted throughout the world. Satan will also plant his people, the sins of the evil one, among God's people to counteract God's truth. The principal work of Satan's emissaries within the visible Kingdom of Heaven will be undermining the authority of the Word of God and promoting unrighteousness and false doctrine.

Christ later spoke of a great deception among His people because of these professed Christians who are really false teachers. The condition of Satan's people existing among God's people will terminate with God's final destruction of all the wicked at the end of age. "It is true that some preach Christ out of envy and rivalry, but others out of goodwill. The later do so in love, knowing that I am put here for the defense of the gospel. Whatever happens conduct yourselves in a manner worth of the gospel of Christ" (Philippines 1:15-16, 27). God gave Apostle Paul the important and sensitive task of defending the Gospel as the Scripture defined it. Likewise, all believers must, and are called to defend the biblical truth of the Scripture and also to resist those, or by resting those who try to distort the faith.

All the believing Christians must stand firm in one spirit, be immovable, they should stand for the true essence of the unity of the Spirit which consists primarily of living in a worthy manner, standing firm in one spirit and in one purpose striving together as a warriors for the defense of the Gospel according to the apostolic revelation and defending Gospel truth against those who are the enemies of the Cross of Christ. These Scriptures say, "Dear friends, although I was very eager to write to you about the salvation we share, I felt I have to write and urge you to contend for the faith that was once for all entrusted to the Saints" (Jude 3). Those who are faithful to Christ are placed under the solemnity obligation to contend for the faith that God delivered to the apostles and to us today. The faith which consists of the gospel proclamation by Jesus Christ and the apostles during His earthly ministry. This was fixed with an unutterable truth by the Holy Scripture that was embodied in the New Testament. We have to see the faith more than an objective truth, but as a way of life, that is to be lived with love, and purity. It is a Kingdom of God that comes in power from Heaven to all the believing Christians in the Holy Spirit. That says all the believers of Jesus Christ must proclaim the gospel of God to all the nations with signs and miracles and with the gift of the Holy Spirit.

The word "contend" means that all the faithful believers must fight in the defense of the faith. Believers must struggle, suffer, labor intensely under great stress, or fight, and exert oneself to the utmost in the defense of God's Word and the New Testament faith, even though it may be costly and agonizing. Believers must deny themselves if it necessary or accept martyrdom for the sake of the gospel of God. Contend for the faith means taking a direct stand against those within the visible church who deny the Bible's authority or distort the ancient faith as presented by Christ and the apostles, and proclaiming it as redemptive truth to all people.

"As for mortals, their days are like grass; they flourish like a flower of the field; for the wind passes over it, and it is gone, and its place knows it no more. But the steadfast love of the Lord is from everlasting to everlasting on those who fear him, and his righteousness to children's children, to those who keep his covenant and remember to do his commandments" (Psalm 103).

Chapter Twenty- Three

The Church: People of Hope

The Church and the hope of glory in Christ's return is a hope that is centered in Christ's return to set up His Kingdom on Earth and live with His people forever. The Scriptures says: "I charge you to keep this command without spot, or blame until the appearing of our Lord Jesus Christ, which God will bring about in his own time. God the blessed and only Ruler, the King of kings and the Lord of lords, who alone is immortal and who lives in an unapproachable light, who no one has seen or can see, to him be honor and might forever Amen" (1st Timothy 6:13b-16).

Apostle Paul told his Christian son, Timothy, to clearly preach Christ's appearing which could happen anytime during his lifetime, or at any time after his lifetime.

New Testament apostles must constantly encourage believers in their generation to expect and hope for the Lord's return in their lifetime. Believers must love the Lord and long for His return and His immediate presence. This must be a basic motivation in the lives of believing Christians. "Now there is in store for me the crown of righteousness, which the Lord, the righteous Judge, will award me on that day and not only to me, but also to all who have longed for his appearing" (2nd Timothy 4:8). It is because of the faithfulness of Apostle Paul to his Lord and to the Gospel entrusted to him, the Holy Spirit witnessed to him that God's loving approval and the crown of righteousness was awaiting him in Heaven.

God has reserved rewards in heaven for all who remain loyal to Christ Jesus and His Gospel. Believers have an intense longing for the Lord's return to take them from the Earth to be with Him forever. "While, we wait for the blessed hope, the glorious appearing of our great God and Savior, Jesus Christ. Who gave himself for us to redeem us from all wickedness and purify for himself a people that are his very own, eager to do what is good" (Titus2:13). Blessed means a fullness of blessing, as well as God's gracious favor and the happiness of being in the new bodies that will be immortal and that will not be subject to corruption, or decay. This great hope is related to the glorious appearance of our Lord and Savior Jesus Christ, which will happen when He returns to His own on Earth.

Believers are to wait for our Lord's appearing with prayers, faith and purity of heart, with fervent desires as a faithful and chosen people. Jesus Christ shed His precious blood on the Cross in order to redeem humanity from all wickedness and the desire to defy the Law of God and the holy standards, to make believers a holy people, separated from sin and death and the world, in order to be used by God as His very own special possession and people. Scripture says: "And if I go prepare a place for you, I will come back and take you to be with me that you also may be where I am. You know the way to the place where I am going" (John 14:3-4). The angel said to the disciples that Christ that was taken away from you today, will be coming back, surely as Jesus Christ went to Heaven. He will return from His Father's presence and take His followers to be with Him in Heaven to the place He prepared for them. This was the hope of all the New Testament Christians as well as the hope of all the believers today.

The main purpose of Christ's return is to set up His Kingdom on Earth so that all those who believe in Him will live with Him forever. Our Lord was referring to the Rapture when He said, "I will take you with me." Christians will be caught up in the clouds to meet with Christ in the air. Christ Jesus coming to His own faithful will enable them to escape the future tribulation and trial that will come upon the Earth. This glorious and eternal reunion of believers and their Lord is a comforting doctrine for all those who believe in Christ, who desire to be with the Lord forever. Therefore, encourage one and another with the words of truth. "So Christ was sacrificed once to take away the sins of many people; and he will appear a second time, not to bear sin, but to bring salvation to those who are waiting for him" (Hebrews 9:28). We see in the Scripture under the Old Testament, old covenant, the Israelites watched intensely for the re-appearance of their High Priest, has entered the heavenly sanctuary to make atonement. Likewise believers, knowing that their High Priest has entered the heavenly sanctuary as their advocate, wait with earnest hope for His reappearing to bring salvation to its completion. All the believing Christians must waited patiently for the Lord's appearing.

Almighty God, Father of all mercies, we your servants give you thanks for all your goodness and loving-kindness to us and to all people. We bless you for our creation, preservation, and all the blessings of this life; but above all for your incomparable love in the redemption of the world by our Lord Jesus Christ, for the means of grace, and for the hope of glory. And, we pray, give us an awareness of your mercies, that with truly thankful hearts we may make known your praises, not only with our lips, but in our lives, by giving up ourselves to your service, and by walking before you in holiness and righteousness all the days of our lives; through Jesus Christ our Lord, to whom, with you and the Holy Spirit, be all honor and glory throughout the ages. Amen, Amen, Amen

(Grace All Denominational prayer Ministry, New York)

Chapter Twenty - Four

The Invisible Church & The Visible Church

The invisible church are the body of Christ who truly believe in Him and are united with Him by their living faith in Him. The invisible church consists of local congregations, which contains the faithful overcomers. The invisible church is the instrument of the Kingdom of God. The Day of Pentecost marked, or opened the beginning of the fulfillment of the Holy Spirit inhabiting the Church. The presence of the Holy Spirit in the life of all believers in the world, which created the Temple of God in our heart. The invisible church is where Jesus Christ is the head of the body, the foundation of the Church and the corner stone, "He is the beginning and the first born from among the dead, so that in everything he might have the supremacy." The invisible churches are those who work fervently in the service of the Lord with great affection for the Lord's service with sincere love, which was wrought in them by the Holy Spirit. "He is the image of the invisible God, the first born over all creation. For by him all things were created; things in heaven and on earth, visible and invisible, whether thrones, or powers, or rulers or authorities; all things were created by him and for him. He is before all things, and in him all things hold together. And he is the head of the body, the church; he is the beginning and the first born from among the dead, so that in everything he might have the supremacy" (Colossians 1:15-18). Jesus Christ is the head; He is the supreme, the ruler Jesus Christ is the heir and the ruler of all creation as the eternal Son, this affirms the creative activity of Jesus Christ. All things in Heaven and on Earth material and spiritual, owe their existence to Jesus Christ work as the active agent in creation for the invisible church and the visible church. All things hold together and are sustained by Him. The invisible churches are the believers that were saved according to the Old Covenant provisions. The invisible church were in dwelt and regenerated by the power of the Holy Spirit before the Day of Pentecost, and the outpouring of the Holy Spirit was an experience which occurred after the regeneration by the Holy Spirit by the believer.

Baptism in the Holy Spirit on the Day of Pentecost was a second and distinctive work of the Spirit in them. All the believing Christians receive the Holy Spirit at the time of their regeneration, or at the time after their conversion. They must experience the baptism in the Spirit that will empower them to be Christ's witness to unbelievers and sinners The invisible church were: "The living stone rejected by men but chosen by God and precious to him you also, like living stones, are being built into spiritual house to be a holy priesthood offering   spiritual sacrifices acceptable to God through Jesus Christ" (1st Peter 2:4-5). Old Testament priesthood was restricted to the descendants of Aaron alone.

The activity of the Old Testament Priests was to offer sacrifices and intercession to God on behalf of His people and they are to communicate with God. But through Christ Jesus, every born again believer has been made a priest before God. The priesthood of all believers means the following - All believers has a direct access to God through Christ; all the believing Christians were obligated to live holy lives. All the invisible church has access to the throne room of grace day and night. Their function is to offer themselves as spiritual sacrifices, which are the presentation of believer's body as a living sacrifice, holy and acceptable to God. This means that activities of spiritual worship - sacrifice of praise means the fruit of our lips giving thankfulness and praises to Him, believers' sacrifices of good works, sacrifices that are pleasing to God.

The Sacrifice of possessions, sharing our material things with or to help others and the sacrifice of service witness and speaks of the gospels of God to the unsaved, both Jews and the Gentiles. The sacrifice of the invisible church are accepted by God through Jesus Christ, only the mediator that can approach God in the first place and Christ is the only one who can make our offerings acceptable to God. Jesus Christ's role as a cornerstone was revealed in the Scripture. He points out that God the Father in His foreknowledge has determined that Jesus Christ will have a unique position, that He is an elect and precious stone; He is dependable, He cannot disappoint those who believe in Him. A cornerstone binds two Walls together and it also symbolizes the foundation on which the entered building rest. Christ as the cornerstone, He is the true and genuine foundation, the one who has united the believing Jews and the Gentile together like two walls in one building, into one new man. Christ is the topmost stone in the world; without Him there would be no strength to the building.

The cornerstone is the only stone occupying the highest place in the structure of the building. It is the only stone that shapes the structure so that Christ, the capstone of the invisible church, the truly unique stone - the invisible church gets its character and behavior from Him. When Christ returns, the building like a pyramid will be completed. The Lord Jesus Christ is the image of the invisible God. An image that means that the Lord Jesus Christ has enabled believers to see what God is like. Our Lord said: "God is a Spirit. Those who worship him must worship him in Spirit and in truth"(John 4:24). The invisible church Scripture says Jesus Christ explained to the Samaritan woman that the worship of God must come from believers' state of mind in which we worship God, it also concerns all believers they must be right, not only in the object of our worship, but very important in the manner of our worship which Jesus was instructing the Samaritan woman.

All true worshipers must worship God in Spirit and in truth as their character and as a duty in their service of the Lord. The visible church is the members of local church, all who are the members of local church are called visible church. The visible church consists of all the elect that have been or shall gather into one under Jesus Christ as the head, the body and the fullness of Him that filled all in all. The visible church is the universal church that is under the teaching of the Gospel. They consist of all those throughout the world profess the true religion, children of God, and the Kingdom of our Lord and Savior, Jesus Christ; they are the house and family of God. The visible and invisible does not mean that Christ has two churches. Jesus Christ builds only one church.

The name visible and invisible are used in order to interpret two distinct aspects of one church whereby all genuine believers are members of the invisible church while they are on Earth or in Heaven, whereever they are, alive or those that have passed away to eternity, or died physically, but spiritually they are with Christ. The people that profess to be Christians, but they are not truly converted are part of the members of visible church. People that truly believe in Jesus Christ claim to have faith, but never give their life to Christ are members of the visible church. They are not truly united with Jesus Christ; they are not part of invisible church. The invisible church cannot be fully known, or distinguished, or discerned by the physical eye of believers. As no one can read the heart of human being to find out if the person is truly in the Lord or not. Some pastors, ministers and reverends were part of visible church; they claim they served the Lord, but they are not in union with him.

The calling of God of individuals is of God's activity and is spiritual. The redemption of God through Jesus Christ is spiritual in saving the human soul. The Holy Spirit of God gives a genuine saving faith to only the elect of God. There are many believers of the Lord Jesus Christ in every denomination. Churches with no believing Christians have the ability to determine, or know who are truly the body of Christ, the elect of God throughout the universe.

All the believing Christians are from one end of the Earth to another. Therefore, what is close to us as believers is open clearly to God, who is the immortal, invisible, the only wise God. God knows who are those that belong to Him. The visible church are designated to be visible, it consists of everyone who professes to be true Christians, everyone who call on the name of Jesus Christ are the visible church, if he has the knowledge of the Gospel profess faith in Christ and repent from his or her sins. Our Lord gave us the parable of wheat and tares, as well as good seed are sown, also good fish and bad fish. People who are visible church members, who never truly believe in Christ receive the outward membership, they are never regenerated or saved, forgiven or unite with Jesus Christ spiritually and they are not sanctified. The members of the visible church preach, teach the gospel, obeyed the outward calls of the gospel, submitting to baptism and place themselves in a high position at the local church.

The true Christians are united to Christ by the power of the Holy Spirit and they can never apostatize while those who are not baptized in the Spirit and not united with Christ can apostatize. Jesus Christ said not everyone who is a member of the visible church on Earth is truly member of the invisible church in Heaven.

"Bless the Lord, O my soul, O Lord my God, you are very great. You are clothed with honor and majesty, wrapped in light as with a garment. You stretch out the heavens like a tent, you set the beams of your chambers on the waters, you make the clouds your chariot, you ride on the wings of the wind, you make the winds your messengers, fire and flame your ministers. You set the earth on its foundations, so that it shall never be shaken. You cause the grass to grow for the cattle, and plants for people to use, to bring forth food from the earth, and wine to gladden the human heart, oil to make the face shine, and bread to strengthen the human heart"
(Psalm 104).

Chapter Twenty - Five

Jesus Christ: the Rock of His Church

Jesus Christ is the Rock of the Church, His body. Beginning from the Old Testament, the Scripture revealed in the Book of Exodus: "I will stand there before you by the rock at Horeb. Strike the rock, and water will come out of it for the people to drink. So Moses did this in the sight of the elders of Israel. And he called the place Massah and Meribah because the Israelites quarreled and because they tested the Lord saying, is the Lord among us or not" (Exodus 17:6-7).

In the New Testament this Rock is identified with Jesus Christ, the spring of living water; as the rock was struck, so was Christ was smitten, bitten, by death on the Cross; as Christ was the source of blessing for Israel, He is the source of blessing and the giver of the Holy Spirit for the Church.

The Scripture revealed in the Book of Isaiah: "But he was pieced for our transgressions, he was crushed for our iniquities; the punishment that brought us peace was upon him; and by his wounds we are healed" (Isaiah 53:5). Christ was crucified because we have sinned and are guilty before God; Christ is our substitute, He took the punishment for us and paid for the penalty for our sins – the penalty of death so that we can be forgiven and have peace with God. By Jesus Christ's wounds we are healed; this healing is referring to salvation with all its benefits, which could be physical or spiritual. Sickness or diseases are the work of Satan's activity in the world. Jesus Christ gave the gifts of healing to His church to heal the sick and part of their proclamation of the Kingdom of God and gospel of God. Jesus Christ is the rock of the Church according to the Scripture: "The Lord said to Moses, take the staff, and you and your brother Aaron gather the assembly together. Speak to that rock before their eyes and it will pour out its water. You will bring water out of the rock for the community so they and their livestock can drink. So Moses took the staff from the Lord's presence, just as he commanded him. He and Aaron gathered the assembly together in front of the rock and Moses said to the, Listen, you rebels, must we bring you water out of this rock? Then Moses raised his arm and struck the rock twice with his staff. Water gushed out, and the community and their livestock drank." (Numbers 20:7-11).

Moses and Aaron were commanded to speak to the rock, not to strike it as they did in Horeb. As a result of Moses' disobedience, he was forbidden to lead the people of God into the land of Canaan, the Promised Land. Moses did not carefully follow the Lord's command even though he was the spiritual leader of God's people, the one through whom God gave the land. Moses' duty and responsibility as a leader was to obey God's words and God's commandment, which was greater because of his greater position and influence; Moses sin was two fold: First, He spoke harshly as if God's glory and power resided in him and his brother Aaron. Secondly, Moses' speaking and acting harshly demonstrated his lack of trust in God; this also showed Moses' lack of faith and obedience. Moreover, Moses failed to treat God as the holy one who is worthy of our adoration and worship.

All the believing Christians, including pastors, ministers and all the body of Christ must learn how to trust the Lord Jesus Christ, our rock of ages; we must learn how to put everything we are going through in His hands. They should read the story of Moses again, and again as a reminder. It is the responsibility of all God's ministers and pastors of the Gospel to obey the Word of God, feed the people with the true Word of God, which is greater than any position. Just as Moses disqualified himself from leading the people of Israel to the Promised Land of Canaan, so also ministers and pastors of today can permanently disqualify themselves from certain areas of leadership by their unfaithfulness to God's commands.

Believing Christians must follow Jesus Christ with the spirit of holiness; they should communicate with our rock every minute and every second, in everything that pertains to life and holiness. Moses struck the rock for lack of unbelief and trust in God; moreover, Moses disobeyed God's command. All the believing Christians today, must trust our Lord and Savior; they must fully believe in Jesus Christ as the rock of ages; that can never be moved, or changed. Jesus Christ never goes back on His Word. Christ is the rock; for He is immutable, immovable, and He is to all that believe in Him and fly to Him an impenetrable shelter, and to all that trust in Him an everlasting foundation. He is the rock of our salvation and eternal life.

First He suffered for us, now we just need to speak to Him. He will do whatever we want, if He knows that what we asked for in prayer is good for us, for other people as well as is going to win sinners and the lost unto His holy hands. Moses and Aaron improvised; they introduced doubt into this miracle. Jesus Christ is the rock of our salvation.

"Come, let us sing for joy to the Lord; let us shout aloud to the rock of our salvation" (Psalm 95:1). Believers must make sure that they worship and praise the Lord, which must be accompanied by the hearts of obedient to the Lord. "He is the rock, his works are perfect, and all his ways are just. A faithful God who does no wrong, upright and just is he" (Deuteronomy 32:4). Jesus Christ's ways are always perfect; His mercy endures forever. Christ's work is perfect. His work of creation was very good; His work of providence will be unfolded at the right time, and when the mystery of God shall be finished, the perfection of His works will appear to all the people of the Universe.

God is to be praised; believers must offer songs of praises, a joyful noise to the Lord. Spiritual joy is the heart and soul of thankful praise. Believers must be able to rejoice in the Lord Jesus Christ our redeemer King and in what He has done in the New Covenant with His people.

Believers must humble, reverence and in holy awe, praise the Lord, our rock of salvation. Believers must speak forth and sing forth His praises of the abundance of the heart filled with love, and joy, and thankfulness. Let us come together to join in singing to the Lord; let us come together before His presence where His people are open to His manifestations of Himself. Jesus, our rock of salvation, is to be praised because He is a great rock, a great God and a Sovereign Lord of all the people on Earth.

Believers must measure, layout and build their life on the solid rock of Jesus Christ according to the Scripture, as they naturally want to make their life better for themselves and everyone around them or everyone in their life such as their children, husband, parents and everyone that is involved in their life. Believers must know that their life is a building for God, which God made in a unique way with various influences that shape them to live a life of God. Jesus Christ is the rock of all believing Christians.

"The Lord lives! Praise be to my rock! Exalted be God, the Rock, my Savior!(2nd Samuel 22:47), "and drank the same spiritual drink; for they drank from the spiritual rock that accompanied them, and that rock was Christ" (1st Corinthians 10:4). God wonderfully provided in a miraculous way water for the children of Israel to drink in the desert. It was real water, but it's a spiritual drink in the sense that it was spiritual refreshment, which was miraculously provided. The Lord was the one giving them this spiritual water in a miraculous way. This rock signified the river that flowed from it and the same that followed the people of Israel. The rock was Jesus Christ, in the sense that He was the one who provided the rock, and He is the one it represents providing living water to His people. Christ still takes care of all those who belong to Him the same way today and He will continue forever.

"For no one can lay any foundation other than the one already laid, which is Jesus Christ. If any man builds on this foundation using gold, silver, costly stones, wood hay or straw, his work will be shown for what it is, because the day will bring it to light. It will be revealed with fire, and the fire will test the quality of each man's work. If what he has built survives, he will receive his reward" (1st Corinthians 3:11-14). Jesus Christ is the rock of our foundation; he warns that the Church, any member of His body, must not tolerate within its fellowship the world's unrighteous practices or the distortion of the biblical truth. Those who build upon the Lord Jesus Christ's rock of foundation gold, silver, and precious stones are those who hold nothing, but force us on Christ and preach the truth as it is in Jesus Christ and they preach nothing else.

They are building upon a good solid rock of foundation. But others that build wood, hay, and stubble on this foundation, even though they acknowledge the foundation, but they depart from the rules and regulations, and from the mind of Christ in many ways, they build upon the good foundation but they cannot abide the test when the day of trial comes. A time is coming says the Lord when every man's work will be made manifest to himself and to others. A day is coming that will show ourselves and that will show our actions in the light of the Lord. Every man's work shall be revealed by fire and the fire shall try every man's work; some men's work will abide the trial; it will show that they not only built regularly and built very well upon it, but the foundation and its superstructure were all of a piece, and such builder will not and cannot fail of reward.

He will have praises and honor on that day and benefit of eternal recompense after. Fidelity in the people of those who believe in Christ will meet with a full reward in a future life on Christ. And the people will see that the Lord is the rock of our foundation from this Earth to Heaven. Jesus Christ is the Church and water of life. The water of life that Jesus has given unto all the believing

Christians shall break forth into springs of living water causing believers to over flow with His love, His joy, and His peace. "But whosoever drinks the water I give him will never thirst. Indeed, the water I give him will become in him a spring of water welling up to eternal life" (John 4:14). Jesus Christ is the believers' water of life- the water that Jesus gave is a spiritual life, which means all those who believe in Jesus must partake of this living water one must drink. This activity of drinking water is not a momentary, single activity; it must be ongoing, a progressive, our repeated drinking. Drinking of the water of life requires regular communion with the source of the living water, Jesus Christ Himself. No one can continue to drink the water of life if he or she becomes severed from the source.

Such people will become, as the Scripture revealed and describes it, "Springs without water: These men are springs without water and mists driven by a storm. Blackest darkness is reserved for them" (2nd Peter 2:17). Genuine children of God believe in the Scripture, what God has said from the Old Testament to the New Testament; they accept all the Bible's miracles and power of God in the life of His people. Miracles in response to God answering prayers and faith of God's people. Jesus Christ is the believers' water of life, whoever partakes of the spirit of grace shall never thirst. He or she will not have nothing more than God, will be filled with more and more of God and they shall never thirst because this water that Christ gives shall be in him a well of water. He can never be reduced to extremity that has in him a fountain of supply and satisfaction. The water will always be ready, for it shall permanently be in him. The believer does not need to be looking for worldly comfort. Believers have in them a well of water, overflowing, ever flowing. It will be springing up, always in motion, it is springing up unto everlasting life; which initiates the aims of gracious actions.

Spiritual life springs up towards its own perfection in eternal life. It will continue springing up till it comes to perfection, eternal life at last. Whoever drinks of Jesus Christ's mercy and blessings will never thirst again. The blessing will fill the heart and it will over flow it. It is like a bubbling fountain, which will continuously over flow, not only in this life, but in eternity. The meaning of springing up into everlasting life shows that the benefits of the water which Christ Jesus gives are not limited to this Earth alone, but will go with believers forever.

All what the Earth can provide is not enough to fill the human's heart. But the blessings which Christ provides not only fill the human heart, but they are too great for any human heart to contain. The pleasure, the material things of this world are temporary, but the pleasure which our Lord Jesus Christ provides goes on in to everlasting life. Believing Christians should rejoice that Jesus Christ is our living water - believe in Him. We will never go thirsty; honor and glory and power belong to Him. He is worthy of all our praises and thankfulness.

"The trees of the Lord are watered abundantly, the cedars of Lebanon that he planted. In them the birds build their nest; the stork has its home in the fir trees. The mountains are for the wild goats; the rocks are a refuge for the Coneys. You have made the moon to mark the seasons; the sun knows it's time for setting. You make darkness, and it is night, when all the animals of the forest come creeping out. O Lord, how manifold are your works! In wisdom you have made them all; the earth is full of your creatures" (Psalm 104).

Chapter Twenty-Six

Jesus Christ's Priestly Prayer for the Church

"After Jesus said this, He looked toward Heaven and prayed: "Father, the time has come. Glorify your Son, that your Son may glorify you. For you granted him authority over all people that he might give eternal life to all those you have given him. Now this is eternal life; that they may know you, the only true God, and Jesus Christ, whom you have sent. I have brought you glory on earth by completing the work you gave me to do. And now, Father, glorify me in your presence with the glory I had with you before the world began.

I have revealed you to those whom you gave me out of the world. They were yours; you gave them to me and they have obeyed your word. Now they know that everything you have given me comes from you. For I gave them the words you gave me and they accepted them. They knew with certainty that I came from you, and they believed that you sent me. I pray for them. I am not praying for the world, but for those you have given me, for they are yours. All I have is yours, and all you have is mine. And glory has come to me through them. I will remain in the world no longer, but they are still in the world, and I am coming to you. Holy Father, protect them by the power of your name – the name you gave me – so that they may be one as we are one. While I was with them, I protected them and kept them safe by that name you gave me. None has been lost except the one doomed to destruction so that Scripture would be fulfilled.

I am coming to you now, but I say these things while I am still in the world, so that they may have the full measure of my joy within them. I have given them your word and the world has hated them, for they are not of the world any more than I am of the world. My prayer is not that you take them out of the world, but that you protect them from the evil one. They are not of the world, even as I am not of it. Sanctify them by the truth; your word is truth. As you sent me into the world, I have sent them into the world. For them I sanctify myself, that they too may be truly sanctified.

My prayer is not for them alone. I pray also for those who will believe in me through their message, that all of them may be one. Father, just as you are in me and I am in you. May they also be in us so that the world may believe that you have sent me. I have given them the glory that you gave me, that they may be one as we are one. I in them and you in me. May they be brought to complete unity to let the world know that you sent me and have loved them even as you have loved me.

Father, I want those you have given me to be with me where I am, and to see my glory, the glory you have given me because you loved me before the creation of the world.

Righteous Father, though the world does not know you, I know you, and they know that you have sent me. I have made you known to them, and will continue to make you known in order that the love you have for me may be in them and that I myself may be in them" (John 17:1-26).

Jesus' prayer for His disciples and all the believers shows that our Lord has the deepest longings for His followers, both then and now. It is also a Spirit inspired example of how all pastors and ministers should pray for their people, and how Christian parents should pray for their children. In terms of praying for those we love and that are under our care, our greatest concern should be that they may know our Lord Jesus Christ and his Word intimately, that God the Father may keep them from the world, from falling away, from Satan and from false teaching that they may constantly possess the full joy of Jesus Christ. That they be holy in thought, deed and character and that they may be one in purpose and fellowship, as demonstrated by Jesus and God the Father.

Christ also pray for believing Christians' protection, joy, sanctification, love and unity within the body of Christ – the Church - those who belong to God, believe in Christ and are separated from the world. He wants them to obey the Word of God, and the commandment of Christ, and accept His teachings and preaching.

Our Lord prays for Himself and sanctifies Himself. Jesus Christ sanctifies Himself by setting Himself apart to do the will of God the Father to die on the Cross. Jesus suffered on the Cross in order that those who believe in Him might be separated from the world and set apart for God forever. Our Lord and Savior Jesus Christ prayed also for the unity of all the body of Christ – the Church which is spiritual unity. Unity based on living in Christ, knowing Him, and experiencing the love of the Father and the fellowship of Jesus Christ.

Believing Christians may lead others to Jesus Christ that they may persevere in the faith and finally be with Christ in Heaven that the love that the Father has for Jesus may be in them, so that they love Jesus with the same fervent love that the Father does, and that Jesus Christ by his Spirit may dwell in and with them. It is a special quality of life that believers receive when they partake of the essential life of God through Christ; this allows them to know God in an ever-growing knowledge and fellowship with the Father, Son and the Holy Spirit.

Jesus prayed for the sanctification of all the believers with the truth – sanctify means to make holy, to separate or set apart for the Lord. Jesus Christ, on the evening before His crucifixion, prayed that His disciples will be a holy people, separated from the world and sin and the sin nature for the purpose of worshiping and serving God the Father.

"Since you call on a Father who judges each man's work impartially, live your lives as strangers here in reverent fear. For you know that it was not with perishable things such as silver or gold that you were redeemed from the empty way of life handed down to you from your forefathers, but with the precious blood of Christ, a lamb without blemish or defect" (1st Peter 1:17-19).

Summary

The Church is known as the body of Christ, also known as the bride of Christ. "Keep watch over yourselves and all the flock of which the Holy Spirit has made you overseers. Be shepherds of the church of God, which he bought with his own blood" (Acts 20:28). The Church consists of only those who by Christ's grace and the fellowship of the Holy Spirit are faithful to the Lord Jesus Christ and to the Word of God; therefore, as a major aspect of guarding God's church, church leaders must discipline and correct with love. The church referred to people of this world assembly of people called together in the New Testament to primarily gather all God's people in Christ, who are called the citizens of the Kingdom for the primary purpose to worship God. The Church can also be referred to a local church or the universal church in which Christ is the head. The Church is also known as the people of God or God's children. The Church is also redeemed believing

Christians who gave their life to Christ through the death, burial and the resurrection of Jesus Christ.

The Church is the member of Jesus Christ who functions as a living standard, in personal relationship with Christ. The Church consists of people whom God consecrated, called out of the world of sin into His glorious Kingdom; separated from the world, having the Lord Jesus as one God and Father.

The role of the Church in this Universe, and the role of all the believers in the body of Christ, must remain in a constant activity of the soul, spirit and body. "So whether you eat or drink or whatever you do, do it all for the glory of God. Do not cause anyone to stumble, whether Jews, Greeks or the church of God - even as I try to please everybody in every way. For I am not seeking my own good but the good of many, so that they may be saved. Follow my example, as I follow the example of Christ" (1st Corinthians 10:31-33).

The main object of the believer's life is to please God and promote His Holy Name, and His glory. Believing Christians must do everything they do for the glory of God, in honor and thanksgiving to Him as our Lord, our creator and our redeemer King. Believers must honor Jesus Christ by obedience, thankfulness, reliance, prayer, faith and loyalty. Do all in the glory of God must be a primary direction of our lives. It should be a guide for our conduct and it should be a test of our actions. All the believing Christians, the body of Christ, the Church must follow the example of Christ Jesus our Lord and have a Christ like character. The teachings were the instructions relating to the doctrine, where moral standard and codes of conduct that were delivered to the church by Apostles Paul through Christ's authority.

"The body is a unit, though it is made up of many parts, and though all its parts are many, they form one body. So it is with Christ. For we were all baptized by one Spirit into one body - whether Jews or Greeks, slave or free - and we were all given the one Spirit to drink." (1st Corinthians 12:12-13). The baptism by one Spirit refers neither to water baptism or Christ's baptism of the believers in the Holy Spirit, such baptizing believers, it is a spiritual transformation that happens at conversion and that puts all the believers in Christ. God unites believers to Jesus Christ as our lead, the Holy Spirit also unites those who believe in Jesus Christ alone to one another so that we who are many become one body of Christ – the Church.

The Scripture has also revealed that God Himself has arranged all the members of the body of Jesus Christ, putting believers in a specific positions and giving them a particular gifts for the good of all the body - just as each organ and member of the human body has its own role and function, each Christian has a calling that is indispensable to the health of the Church. The body of Christ, the Church, is a spiritual body. The Church is spiritual made up of believers who have submitted to Christ in faith and in obedience. The body of Christ is not in the flesh, but in the Spirit. The church must learn how to value every member because each one contributes in so many ways whether we see it or not, there are some with speaking talent, the other, a church leader of a local church they all contributed to the welfare of the Church.

Christ is the head of the body, the head always regulates and directs the body; the rest of the body follows the decisions the head makes. It means clearly that the head rules the body. Christ as the head of the church, the head has all authority in Heaven and on Earth to rule the body. Jesus Christ is the Savior of the body the Church.

"Yonder is the sea, great and wide, creeping things innumerable are there, living things both small and great. There go the ships and Leviathan that you formed to sport in it. These all look to you to give them their food in due season. May the glory of the Lord endure forever; may the Lord rejoice in his works who looks on the earth and it trembles, who touches the mountains and they smoke. I will sing to the Lord as long as I live; I will sing praise to my God while I have being. Bless the Lord, O my soul. Praise the Lord"

(Psalm 104).

My Prayer for the Churches

God the Father Almighty, you are the maker of Heaven and the Earth, the sea and everything that dwells in it. Jesus Christ the only begotten Son of the Father full of grace and truth, the Holy Spirit, ever one God. Lord Jesus Christ you are the foundation, the cornerstone, the head of the church, you are the immortal, the invisible and the only wise God. You are the way the truth and the life; in you all life consists. Lord Jesus Christ you said all churches must be one in you as you and Father are one; you also told Thomas in the Scripture: "Then Jesus told him, Because you have seen me, you have believed; blessed are those who have not seen and yet have believed" (John 20:29).

Lord Jesus Christ you also told Apostle Peter that: "You will build your church and all the gates of hell will not prevail against it. I call unto you; with my spirit, soul and body today and as long as I will live on this Earth to help us with your divine love, mercy, and especially with the authority of Your Word; bring great changes to all your churches on this Earth, beginning from the Old Testament to the New Testament churches to the smallest churches right from the womb churches that lives in the mountain; visible and invisible churches, as well as churches that live under the Earth. We are part of Your body, Your flesh and Your bones. Bring us together in one before Your second coming our Lord and Savior. Make all the churches to make unceasing prayer to you every day, every minute as part of your body help us to have one form of worship. Help all your body to worship you in Spirit and in truth. And pray for Your body on Earth, the prayer that can never be uttered. I worship you in Spirit and in truth. I pray for your churches on Earth, the prayer that can never be uttered. Jesus Christ you are the same yesterday, today and forever. You are the one and only the foundation of the Church. You are the rock of the Church, the only one church of Jesus Christ the Son of God, You gave Your life to the Church our Lord; You are the Husband of the church, we are your Bride, you are the Head of the church and the Corner-Stone, chosen and precious, binding the churches in one on Earth and in Heaven. You said: "God is a Spirit, and those who worship Him must worship Him in Spirit and in truth" (John 4:24). Our Lord Jesus Christ you explained this truth to the Samaritan woman that the worship of God must come from our state of mind in which we worship God the Father, with all our efforts and show our concerns to be in the right relationship with You, not only in the object of our worship, but very important in the manner of our worship which was instructed the Samaritan woman that all worshipers must worship God in Spirit and in truth as their character and as their duty. Help all your church on Earth to be able to worship you and the Father and Holy Spirit and in truth.

Let all those who believe in You give their lives to You in Spirit and in Truth. Help all the believers to worship the Father in Spirit and in truth. Send your Holy Angels, all the heavenly host, and the body of Christ in Heaven to straighten out all our problems, trouble, persecution, afflictions, spiritual attack from the enemy in different ways around the world. Be our guide and let us know that you are the Ever- Living God, the Head of the Church; we are part of Your body, Your flesh and Your bones. Correct all Your body, the churches, help us to be one in You and in one in everything that pertains to the Gospel of God. Correct all the false preachers that are causing confusion among the body of Christ. You are the God of resurrection eternal life, no one before You and there is no one after; continue to help us to build your church on this Earth and do not let the gates of Hades prevail against it. Fulfill the Great Commission through all the body of Christ the believers on this Earth, perform your great miracle through us, exhibit your infinite power through us, exercise your infinite love through us to the people of this world.

Turn all the false teachers, false preachers, false prophets around and let them preach the true Gospel boldly and clearly to all their congregations. They are making thousands of congregations, but they are not teaching the true Word of God that will convert the soul. Lord Jesus Christ, turn all your enemies to Your friends. Those nations that they don't want Christians to preach the Gospel of God, turn them around; let them be lovers of God and His Gospel. Let Your holy name be magnified, glorified, adored in the heart and minds of every living soul on the Earth. Turn evil to good, turn violence to peace, turn wickedness to love, turn jealously and envy to love. Let all the people of this world help each other and help each other beginning from their neighborhood, city, states and the entire country and between the nations. Lord Jesus Christ let those who do not know You, seek You and find You; let them give their life to You, spirit, soul and body, in total surrender to Your Lordship where they can be protected and worship you who only is the head of the body.

Empower all your church to preach, teach with the power of the Holy Spirit. Let the gospel of God rush into all the people in all the nations and make them alive in You, our living Savior. We are waiting for Your return You are our hope of glory; come quickly Lord Jesus Christ. You are continuously forgiving the sinners and the lost, people of all other religions, atheists and everyone in the world, if they come to you with a repentant heart, hear their prayers and forgive them their sins no matter how gruesome it is, wash them as white as snow. Protect all the Christians that were being persecuted for their faith; let the people of the persecuting nations makes a good decision to release the persecuted Christians from their prisons; release them as you released Apostle Peter from the prison through your Angel. Perform your miracle, release all the persecuting Christians so that they can come out and continue to serve You in spirit and in truth with singleness of heart. Lord Jesus Christ fulfill the Great Commission through all the believers, purify us with Your Word, Your Word is true.

In Your Matchless, Great Mighty Holy Name, I pray accept my prayers amen, amen, amen.

"Now that you have purified yourselves by obeying the truth so that you have sincere love for your brothers, love one another deeply, from the heart. For you have been born again, not of perishable seed, but of imperishable, through the living and enduring word of God" (1st Peter 1:22-23).

Hymn of Adoration

Praises to Christ, the Head of The Church

Christ whose glory fills the skies, Christ, the true, the only light, Sun of righteousness arise, triumph over shades of night: Day-spring from on high, be near, Day-star, in my heart appear!

Dark and cheerless is the dawn till your glories shine on me; joyless is the day's return till your mercy's beams I see: as they inward light impart, cheer my eyes and warm my heart.

Visit then this soul of mine; pierce this gloom of sin and grief; fill me, radiancy divine, scatter all my unbelief: more and more yourself display, shining to the perfect day!

Biblical Indexes

Genesis 1:1-2, 12:4, 28:18, 22, 28: 20, 31:13, 35:2, 17:9-10, 12:8, 13:4, 24:12, 25:21, 18:22-33, 20:7, 2:3

Exodus 6:6-7, 12:14-15, 15:18, 20:8-11, 23:14-17, 30:7-9, 28:6-7, 20:1-2, 20:11

Leviticus 23:15-17, 19:2, 1:7, 16:29, 1:8, 27:30-3220:14

Numbers 20:7-11, 27:21

Deuteronomy 9:10, 4:32-40, 31:9-13, 33:8, 20:2, 10:8, 31:9, 27:14-15

1st King 18:41-46, 8:11, 8:11, 8:57

2nd King 5:1, 10, 14

1st Chronicles 16:36

2nd Chronicles 5:11-14

Job 1:5, 42:6, 42:8-9, 6:8-9

Psalms 127:1, 2:7, 115:18, 103:1-2, 86:11, 145:18, 99:1-9, 103:2, 78:12, 92:1, 5:3,
66:13-15

Isaiah 53:12, 54:5-6, 4:4, 53:12, 42:1, 66:2, 57:15, 14:24-27

Ezekiel 36:25-27, 40:48, 14:3-7, 10:18

Daniel 9:3-4

Joel 2:23-28

Matthew 13:23, 15:13-14, 3:11, 7:19, 16:17-19, 3:7-9, 3:13-17, 16:18, 18:15-17, 26:26-29, 6:24, 23:13, 29, 35, 17: 1-2, 20-21, 22:16-22, 6:5-7, 8:5-7, 10-12, 17:20-21, 24:24- 25, 13:22, 11:28-30, 16:18b, 28:18-20,

Mark 10:13-16, 1:8, 11:15-19, 1:40-45, 2:27-28

Luke 24:25-27, 11:13, 19:10, 22:32-34, 22:19-20, 4:16, 24:1, 7:11-15

John 3:16-18, 1:12-13, 8:29, 31-32, 17:1-26, 1:30-34, 14: 3-4, 17, 20:22, 9:11, 19:34. 3: 1-3, 5, 8, 1:32-34, 4:23-24, 6:35, 14:6, 14:12-14, 14:15-19, 20:21-22, 13:4-5, 13: 14- 17, 20:29, 17:21, 4:24

Acts 1:5, 9:13-14, 1:4-5, 8, 2:1-4, 14, 2:8-11, 2:33, 38, 12:5, 2:46, 42, 4:30-31, 3:1-10, 5:12, 16, 8:6, 4:32-33, 4:29, 2:47, 16:8, 12:5, 12, 13:3, 19: 32,39,41, 7:38, 1:5, 11:16, 1:15-17, 20:7, 1:14, 15:1-35, 2:38, 3:16, 26:18, 20:28, 6:8

Romans 3:21-24, 3:21-24, 8:26-29, 8:34, 12:4-5,8:2-5, 12:1-2, 6-7, , 10:9-13, 6:3-5, 8:9-11, 15:4-6, 4:16-25, 14:1- 4, 6:1-4, 1:16-17

1st Corinthians 1:7, 1:30-31, 1:2, 11:1, 15:45-46, 3:1-4, 12:13, 10:16-17, 31-33, 12:12-13,   11:27-29, 12:1-11, 11:17-22, 12:1,28-31, 4-11, 14:27-28, 11:23-26

2nd Corinthians 13:14, 5:17, 6:16, 11:2,

Galatians 2:20, 3:1-4, 3:3

Ephesians 4:11, 6:17-18, 6:11-15, 5:23, 2:19-205:25-27, 1:4-6, 4:12-13, 4:4-6, 4:1-3, 1:21-22, 4:4-6

Philippians 1:15-16

Colossians 1:15-18, 2:11-12, 1:18-20

2nd Thessalonians 1:8-9

1st Timothy 5:10, 3:15, 6:13b-16,

Titus 2:13, 3:5-7

Hebrews 9:28, 7:25, 4:15, 10:25, 10:9, 13:15-16

James 2:4

1st Peter 2:4-5, 1-7, 2:4-10, 2:5, 1:2

1st John 2:1, 5:6-12, 3:4-5

Jude 17-20

Revelation 21:1-5

BIBLIOGRAPHY

<u>Archaeological Study Bible - An Illustrated Walk through Biblical History and Culture</u> (1978) by International Bible Society Zondervan Publishing House Grand Rapids, Michigan.

<u>Believer's Bible Commentary A Complete Bible Commentary In One Volume</u> by William MacDonald Edited by Art Farstad (1917) Thomas Nelson Publishers Nashville, Tenn.

<u>Evangelical Dictionary of Biblical Theology</u> edited by Elwell (1973) Baker Books, A division of Baker Book House Co. Grand Rapids, Michigan.

<u>Exploring The New Testament</u> by Ralph Earle, Th. D Editor Harvey J. S. Blaney, Th. M Carl Hanson, Th. D. 1955 Beacon Hill Press Kansas City, Mo.

<u>Matthew Henry's Commentary In One Volume</u> by Matthew Henry Edited by Rev, Leslie F. Church, Ph,D (1960) Zondervan Publishing House Grand Rapids, Michigan.

<u>The Student Bible</u> by Philip Yancey and Tim Stafford (1994)   Zondervan Publishing House Grand Rapids, Michigan.

Books previously Published by the author:
Grace Dola Balogun
by
Grace Religious Books Publishing & Distributors, Inc. New

York

PRAYER THE SOURCE OF STRENGTH FOR LIFE -
English Edition

Prayer the Source of Strength for Life is a powerful book that will energize your spirit to pray more and more until the prayer is part of your life and until the gate of Heaven is opened and your prayer is answered. Your prayer life will change your life.

LA ORACION FUENTE DE FORTALEZA PARA LA VIDA – Spanish Edition.

Dios no's dio el poder de la oracion, quiere que lo usemos; debemos illamar, comunicarnos con el en todo lo que estemo spasando. El espera saber denosotros.

Spirit Power Volumes I and II

Spirit Power Volumes I and II both discuss the power of the Holy Spirit in the lives of believers.

The Power of the Spirit of God begins from the creation of the world up until today. That power will also continue until Christ returns to reign. Hallelujah

THE CROSS AND THE CRUCIFIXION

Our Lord Jesus Christ died on the Cross to bring forth love and compassion. Sin's impact on human life brings all other evil into our world, from one society to another society, from one culture to another.

But in Christ, we are clothed with His holiness. We have the gift of eternal life. The gate of Heaven is open and we are eligible for our inheritance in Heaven.

Hallelujah! Hosanna in the Highest. Jesus Christ paid it all, unto Him all we owe. The Cross of Christ is the Cross of joy, peace, and righteousness to all who believe in Him.

THREE SIMPLE SOLUTIONS FOR WORLD PEACE

Three Simple Solutions for World Peace is a book that clears all the confusion that many people of the world have been going through for many years. It is a book that gives light and advice to some of the problems that plague the world, and that offers solutions for these problems. It is a book that is full of knowledge, understanding and solutions that will bring some peace to the world.

Justification by Faith Alone in Christ Alone

Justification by Faith Alone in Christ Alone will clear all the confusion of believers' faith in Jesus Christ. Believers will also rejoice in the long sufferings – they will rejoice in their sufferings, afflictions, persecutions, rejections and all various trials that may press in on them because these long-sufferings will help all the believers to be redeemed in Christ.

CHRISTIAN CELL PHONE SERIES:

Christian Cell Phone Godly Wisdom helps readers understand the role of God's wisdom and the importance of obtaining godly wisdom in one's life to produce prosperous results in all areas of life. These areas are critical and include family, relationships and finances. The acquiring of God's wisdom is to be sought after in life and will impact others as well.

Christian Cell Phone God's Favor is designed to give readers knowledge of God's favor from the Old Testament to the New Testament. With an analysis of the favor that was on Jesus, the Son of God, the reader will find that God's favor can completely change one's life and lead others to Christ as well.

Christian Cell Phone God's Anointing takes a look at the anointing on the life of Jesus that includes present day believers in Christ Jesus. This anointing can be applied to all areas of life and can be seen in miraculous ways. The anointing is what makes our life incredible and supernatural, drawing all those who see, to Christ.

JESUS CHRIST THE JOY OF CHRISTMAS

Jesus Christ the Joy of Christmas gives praise and tribute to the child that was born in Bethlehem. Tracing the prophecies of Old about this King that was born, the author gives an account of the sinless Lamb of God who came to take away the peoples' sin from a biblical perspective, who is the real Joy of Christmas.

Grace D. Balogun

PRAYER FOR THE BULLY VICTIMS AND THE BULLY TOO!

Prayer for the Bully Victims and the Bully Too addresses the issue of the bully from the classroom to the home. By the use of scriptural application, the author takes a look at what can be done to help the bully kid and their victims. The author has written several key prayers that readers can use to help either the bully victim or parents who are dealing with a child that has become a bully.

I AM THE RESURRECTION AND THE LIFE

I Am The Resurrection and The Life: Powerful, inspirational and written from a firm biblical perspective, multi-published author Grace Dola Balogun, gives life to others through the power of Jesus Christ who is the Resurrection and the life. This book will open eyes to the amazing and abundant blessings of accepting Jesus Christ as your Lord and Savior, giving keen insight into the Scriptures on the power available to all through the Holy Spirit with an emphasis on aspects of eternal life for the believer.

Grace D. Balogun

I AM THE ETERNAL LIFE

I Am The Eternal Life: Encouraging, uplifting and filled with a sound biblical perspective, this book encourages believers and non-believers alike to look to the One that is Jesus Christ, the Son of God, who is the Bread of life and the one who gives eternal life to all who believe in Him. This book gives readers a heavenly perspective on their life, revealing believer's God-given destiny and purpose to all who call on Jesus Christ as their Lord and Savior. The truth of the Gospel and the Good News is eloquently displayed in this delightful and insightful read.

HE WHO BELIEVES IN ME SHALL NEVER DIE

He Who Believes In Me Shall Never is a fascinating teaching, revealing Jesus as the way, the truth and the life - the Everlasting life. All who believe in Him shall never die. Beginning from the Old Testament, the author takes a look at the fall of humanity through the sin of disobedience through Adam and Eve. Comparing this fall to the sin of disobedience today, the author reveals scriptural truths in the lives of Enoch, Elijah and Moses. The author gives insight into the baptism of the Holy Spirit and gives examples of the Spirit's power and the purpose for which the power is given to believers. The author has given key scriptural insights that all who believe in Jesus Christ will have everlasting life in Him that continues to Heaven.

FORGIVE OUR DEBTS AS WE FORGIVE OUR DEBTORS

Forgive Our Debts As We Forgive Our Debtors speaks of divine forgiveness from the Lord and the Lord's commandment to forgive others, including ourselves. With the Lord's Prayer as a foundation, author Grace D. Balogun, explores from the Old Testament to the New Testament meanings of forgiveness and the consequences of sin. The author gives keen biblical insight into the subject of forgiveness, bringing life-changing healing that is only acquired through the power of forgiveness.

She must be Silent: The Great Commission Bestowed on Both Men and Women is a controversial book that takes a look at the role of women throughout biblical history and gives key scriptural insight into the role of women from the Old Testament to the New Testament. An encouraging, enlightening read, this book is recommended for women and men that want to understand the role of women from a biblical perspective. This book does an excellent job in giving insight into key roles that women play in God's redemptive plan and sheds light on the empowerment of the Holy Spirit that is given to both men and women by God, who is no respecter of persons.

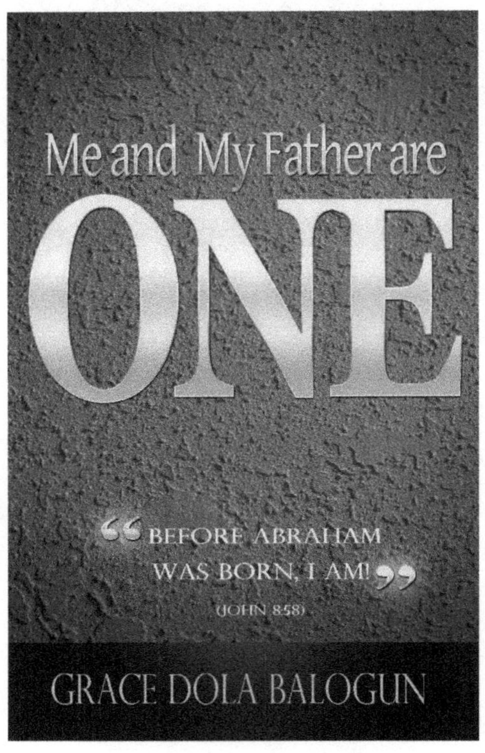

Me and My Father Are One: Before Abraham was Born, I Am (John 8:58) explains that God the Father and Jesus Christ are one from the beginning. In this book, the reader will learn that the plan of redemption is from the Father and is carried out through His Son, Jesus Christ, who is the Word of God. In the beginning, before Abraham, before Adam and Eve, Christ says, "I Am." Written from a biblical perspective, the author displays that Jesus Christ was in the beginning and as Scripture says, "He is before all things, and in him all things hold together" (Colossians 1:17).

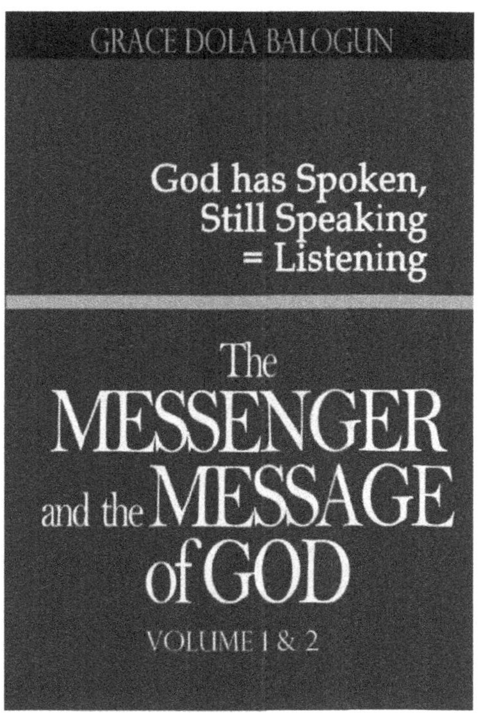

The Messenger and the Message of God (Volumes 1 & 2) systematically offers the message of God spoken through the prophets of Old and Christ's disciples in the gospels, to include the mission of Paul the Apostle. For use as an individual study or within a group setting, these volumes are recommended to gain understanding of certain books of the prophets and the New Testament gospels. *Volume I* is focused on selected prophets of the Old Testament and *Volume II* relates the disciples and their callings in the gospels of the New Testament. God has spoken, is still speaking today and we are to listen to Him, heeding the message.

Be Holy for I Am Holy - God has created and redeemed all of the Christian believers; we belong to Him, and we have passed through troubles and afflictions. We will not be destroyed, for He is with us. We are precious and honored in His sight; believers are the objects of His great love. God loved us before he put us in the womb and brought us into this world. God will never forsake His people. He would continue His love for they would still be a special people reserved for mercy. The expressions of God's goodwill to His people here speak abundance of comfort to all of the spiritual children of upright Jacob who are praying for Israel. Through God's care and concern for His people, God created the people of Israel especially for Himself. He made them into a people; God incorporated them by His covenant—purchased and redeemed them. It is the same way with those who are redeemed by the blood of His Son, Jesus Christ.

Christ's Life in the Life of Christians - This book will help you to understand your position in Jesus Christ as a Christian. Reading this book will also give clear understanding of who Christ is in the life of believing Christians. It will give you more divine ability as well as the power of the indwelling of the Holy Spirit that Christ gave to all who believe and gave their life to Him. Jesus Christ is the one who initiates and the one who establishes the New Covenant and His heavenly ministry is far beyond and far more superior to the ministry of Old Testament priests. The New Covenant is an agreement, promise, the last will and testament and a statement of intention to be bestow divine grace and blessing on all those who believe in God; those who in sincere repentance and through faith accept Jesus Christ as the true Son of God.

Remember the Poor & Needy Among Us will help all the believing Christians to learn how important it is to give to the poor, the needy and the sick. Christians must give part of what God provides for them to increase the work of the Lord on this Earth, to reach the people of the entire world for Jesus Christ in their own language. Christians must set apart for God every day, part of their income, and other natural resources to honor God and to enhance the work of the Kingdom of God on this Earth. They must also give their resources to charity, to the poor, so that the poor may have something to eat and be satisfied. When you make a feast, or doing any celebration, invite the poor and the needy. People who are unable to pay you back because they were unable to work for a living. By feeding them, clothing them, helping them, these types of charity are the true charity.

ABOUT THE AUTHOR

Grace Dola Balogun graduated from Fordham University Graduate School of Religion and Religious Education in the year 2010 with an M.A. in Religion and Religious Education. She has been a prayer mentor and advisor for many Christians of all denominations for many years.

Visit her online at: www.Gracereligiousbookspublishers.com

Grace's Blog: http://author-grace-dola-balogun.blogspot.com/

Facebook - https://www.facebook.com/grace.d.balogun

Twitter - https://twitter.com/prayersource

To order additional copies of this book, please E-mail: info@gracereligiousbookspublishers.com.

This book may also be ordered from 30,000 wholesalers, retailers, and booksellers in the U. S., and in Canada and over100 countries globally.

To contact Grace Dola Balogun for an interview or a speaking engagement, please E-mail:

info@gracereligiousbookspublishers.com

The Spirit and the bride say,

"Come!" And let the one who hears say, "Come!" Let the one who is thirsty come;

and let the one who wishes take the free

gift of the water of life (Revelation 22:17).

MARANATHA EVEN SO COME LORD JESUS (1ST CORINTHIANS 16:22, REVELATION 22:20)

<u>ORDER FORM</u>

TO ORDER YOUR COPY OF ANY BOOK:

NAME:_________________________________

ADDRESS:_________________________________

____

TELEPHONE:_________________________________

FAX#:_________________________________

MAIL:_________________________________

QUANTITY:_________________________________

<u>MAIL TO:</u>

Grace Religious Books Publishing & Distributors, Inc.
New York
213 Bennett Avenue
New York, NY 10040